TH
BLACK FINGER MAN

JACKSON BLACKMORE

Copyright © Jackson Blackmore 2025

All rights reserved.

No part of this publication may be altered, reproduced, distributed, or transmitted in any form, by any means, including, but not limited to, scanning, duplicating, uploading, hosting, distributing, or reselling, without the express prior written permission of the publisher, except in the case of reasonable quotations in features such as reviews, interviews, and certain other non-commercial uses currently permitted by copyright law.

Disclaimer:
This is a work of fiction. All characters, locations, and businesses are purely products of the author's imagination and are entirely fictitious. Any resemblance to actual people, living or dead, or to businesses, places, or events is completely coincidental.

For Shug.

Chapter 1

A young couple sat together in the playground, watching their two kids playing happily on the equipment.

"Do you think we can afford it?" Jennifer asked. "It needs a lot of work…"

"Yeah, of course we can," David replied. "We've come this far in life, and we work hard, so why not just go for it?" he pointed out. "Besides, I'm pretty handy with a hammer," he added with a big grin.

Jenn smiled. "You're right – let's just go for it!"

"Of course I'm right. Even when I'm wrong, I'm right," David said with a smile, causing Jenn to laugh at his very poor impression of Al Pacino from *Donnie Brasco*.

Jenn's laugh, however, soon turned into a cough.

David put his arm around her and kissed her gently on the head. "I'll call the estate agent in the morning and put in our cheeky little offer. According to the home report, it hasn't been rewired since the '80s, so hopefully we can get something knocked off the asking price."

Jenn smiled again, though this was also interrupted by her coughing loudly.

"I think you need to go to the doctor and get that cough looked at, Jenn," David told her, concern in his voice. "You've had it for a while now…"

"I know," she replied, shrugging casually. "It comes and goes. I'll be OK; I'm probably just getting another cold."

David stared at her, frowning, unconvinced.

After months of house-hunting and several fruitless viewings, David and Jenn Sweeney had finally found a house they both loved. It was a 1930s property in the suburbs, with good transport links and great schools nearby. It was also the perfect location for both their jobs.

David worked primarily in the east end of the city as a community-based physiotherapist with the NHS, a job that involved partly working from home – an added bonus. Jenn, a social worker, also worked mainly in the east end, though she occasionally covered other districts.

The couple had first met as students at university – they'd been introduced in the student union bar and had been together ever since. With similar interests and the same taste in music, they often attended concerts together.

One band they both particularly loved was Madness; they would go to see them whenever the band came to town, which was every two years or so. Their favourite Madness song was the band's cover of 'It Must Be Love.'

Eventually – after they'd both graduated – David and Jenn got married and had two kids: Bella, who was six, and Olivia, who was three. They had bought their first home a few years before Bella was born – a small, ground-floor, two-bedroom flat. It wasn't much, but it was theirs, and they were happy living there together.

When Bella came along, the flat started to feel a little cramped, so they moved – this time, into a modest three-bedroom end-terraced house. They loved that house, which was in pretty good condition; all they had to do was paint Bella's bedroom and lay some carpets. On top of that, the area was nice, the neighbours were friendly, and it really felt like a close-knit community.

With their new home and their little family, they felt like they'd won the lottery.

They lived there happily for quite a while, and soon enough, little Olivia was born – at which point it was time for a bit of a switch-around in the house. The couple gave the master bedroom to Olivia and Bella to share, while David and Jenn took the room next door. The box room was turned into a playroom, packed full of toys.

However, as the girls grew older, the young couple began to feel that, yet again, they needed a bigger house. Another deciding factor was the area they lived in – it had changed significantly over the years and no longer felt the same. Most of their elderly neighbours had passed away, and the families who moved in seemed less desirable; loud, drunken parties became a regular occurrence nearly every weekend.

With neither David nor Jenn liking the way things were heading, they decided it was time for a fresh start.

So, David called the estate agent and submitted their offer, which was accepted almost immediately. The house had been on the market for many years, and although it had fallen into slight disrepair, it was still habitable. David and Jenn were delighted that their offer had been accepted; they couldn't wait to get the keys and start renovating.

Once they moved in, they realised just how much work needed doing to it: new electrics, a new boiler, a new kitchen, redecoration throughout, new carpets and flooring, and tidying up the garden and driveway. Fortunately, none of this hard work bothered the young couple – they both knew this was their forever home and were eager to put their own stamp on it, no matter how much time and energy it took.

The property was a large ex-council house with huge front and back gardens. The driveway was monoblocked, though it had become uneven over time, with many of the blocks now sunken and weeds growing through the cracks.

There was also a garage – a separate outbuilding that had been built at the same time as the house. It had been pebbled-dashed and painted white many years ago but now it just looked old and tired, with cracks in the walls and missing concrete in places. To make matters worse, it had a very old asbestos roof that was now covered in moss and grime.

Behind the garage was an old, rusty iron gate with peeling black paint that led around to the back garden.

As you entered the front door of the house, the living room was to the left. It was spacious, with the original fireplace and a single-glazed, hexagon-shaped, lead-lined porthole window facing the driveway. To the right of the hallway, a grand staircase led upstairs. Straight ahead, past the living room, was the kitchen, which – like most of the house – was old and tired. However, it opened up into a fairly modern, spacious extension that had been added roughly 20 years ago. This extension served as a combined dining and living area. It was airy, with plenty of natural light streaming in, and featured a glass PVC door that opened onto the back garden. To the right of the kitchen was a pantry-style cupboard, which led to a narrow corridor extending under the stairs and into a small utility room.

Continuing up the grand staircase, there was a narrow landing. To the left was a fair-sized, semi-modernised family bathroom. The suite itself was modern, with a jacuzzi-style bath and a sleek shower cubicle. Unfortunately, the hideous brown and cream marble tiles rather ruined the overall look. Directly across from the bathroom was another fairly good-sized bedroom. This only needed a lick of paint and some new carpet or laminate flooring. Next to that was a smaller bedroom – a space that appeared even tinier due to the huge, ugly, brown fitted wardrobe that dominated half the room, distorting its depth and making it feel cramped. Lastly, there was the box room, and while small, it had plenty of potential. Access to the loft was in this room via aluminium ladders.

The previous owners had been granted planning permission to convert the attic into an additional bedroom, and – by the looks of it – they had already started the work. All that remained was to install a staircase and complete the decorating.

The attic itself was a good-sized room. The previous owners had cleverly built storage space into the eaves, which helped the space feel larger, as well as making it far more practical.

As soon as their offer on the new house was accepted, David and Jenn put their current home on the market. Their estate agent predicted it would sell quickly due to its location in a nice area and its near-perfect condition. After all, apart from a little paint or wallpaper changes to suit the new buyer's taste, no major renovations were needed.

In the end, the house sold within a week and even fetched £10,000 over the asking price. David and Jenn were over the moon; with their savings and the additional profit from the sale, they could tackle the renovations on the new house and hopefully still have a little money left over for themselves.

Their moving-in date was set for the 17th of January. They couldn't get the keys until the afternoon, which wasn't ideal, but such are the challenges of being locked into a chain while moving house. Fortunately, David and Jenn were at the end of the chain, as their new house had been empty for years. So, despite the usual stresses of moving house with two young children, they remained positive and took it all in their stride.

David's mum, Angela, was a retired psychologist with a free-spirited, eccentric, hippy-type personality. She was deeply into spiritual practices like crystal healing, Reiki, meditation, and everything that came with them. In her house, Angela preferred all her picture frames, mirrors, and various pieces of artwork to hang at slightly crooked angles, as she liked to be 'different.' She had always been a hippy at heart, but her passion for spiritual healing and crystal therapy hadn't fully developed until after the death of David's father, Peter.

Peter had tragically passed away when David was young, following a long battle with cancer. Both Angela and David struggled to cope with the loss, each finding their own ways to deal with it.

For David, the solution was to set goals for himself and work tirelessly to achieve them – anything to keep his mind occupied and away from the pain. Angela's way of coping was more unconventional. Her spiritual practices and eccentric habits might have seemed unusual to some, but David simply humoured her and let her get on with it.

She was happy, and that was all that mattered to him.

***

Soon enough, it was moving day, and David and Jenn arrived at their new house with the removal men and van following closely behind. David parked their car – which was full to the brim with various boxes, as well as their pets – further down the street so the removal van could reverse into the driveway, making it easier to unload the furniture and larger items.

Jenn stepped out of the car and looked up at the house, a big smile spreading across her face. Turning to David, who had opened the boot and was already picking up a box, she said, "I forgot how big the house was."

"Yeah, it's a good size. Just as well it's our forever home – I don't want to be doing this all over again," he replied with a grin as he walked past, carrying the box.

Jenn went to the boot and picked up another box while David walked up the driveway, opening the door for the moving men and instructing them where to put the various items.

As she turned to follow him, Jenn noticed a black jackdaw perched on the front garden pillar where the metal gates were attached. Its piercing green eyes seemed to bore into her, making her stop in her tracks and gasp. The bird twisted its head, staring at her intently with each eye in turn, occasionally squawking and chirping.

A sudden wave of unease washed over her.

Just then, David came back outside to grab another box, walking past the bird without even noticing it. The jackdaw's beady little eyes followed his every move.

When he reached Jenn, he frowned. "Are you OK? You look like you've seen a ghost."

Jenn snapped out of her trance. "Yes, I'm fine," she said quickly. "I was just looking at that black bird sitting on our garden pillar – that's a bad omen, you know."

David turned to glance at the pillar, his frown deepening. "What black bird?" he asked. "I can't see anything."

Jenn looked around wildly, sighing in frustration. "There was a jackdaw! Right there! A black bird with green eyes… it was sitting on our front pillar at the start of the driveway. You walked right past it!" She shook her head. "I'm telling you, seeing a black bird on your property when you move in is a bad omen!"

David rolled his eyes and tutted. "You and your superstitions – God knows where you get all this stuff from. I didn't see any black birds because I'm more concerned with getting the car and van unloaded." He sighed.

"Look, it's obviously flown away now, so we're all good, yeah?" he added, his tone laced with sarcasm as he gave her an exaggerated thumbs-up.

Jenn stared at him for a moment, annoyed, then broke into a smile. "You can be a right sarcastic arsehole sometimes, you know that?"

David grinned. "Yeah, I know – that's why you love me," he said with a wink as he hefted another heavy box from the boot of the car.

Jenn chuckled, walking up the driveway and into the house.

***

David had just finished stacking the last of the boxes in the front living room, while Jenn was attempting to organise the twenty or thirty boxes already surrounding her. She piled them into groups based on the room names written on them, ready to be moved to their proper places later on.

Angela, David's mum, had happily agreed to help by taking the children out for a few hours while they moved in.

David glanced out of the living room window and saw her car pulling into the driveway. A moment later, Angela stepped out and began unbuckling the kids from their car seats. Then, holding their hands, she skipped up to the house with them. "Come on, my little cherubs! Show me your lovely new house!" she announced.

In response, the children squealed with laughter.

"Hello?" Angela called out as she reached the front door.

"We're in here, Mum – in the front living room!" David replied.

Angela and the kids burst into the room, brimming with excitement.

"Mummy!" the girls exclaimed in unison as they ran towards Jenn.

"Hello, my gorgeous little bunnies!" Jenn gushed, kneeling down to hug them. "How are you? Did you have fun with Granny?"

"Yeah!" Olivia replied, beaming. "We went to soft play and Granny got us slushies! Then we went for a drive in her car!"

"Oh wow, that's fantastic!" Jenn smiled. "Granny loves getting you two hyped up on sugar, doesn't she?"

"Well, that is a granny's job," Angela grinned, winking as the kids giggled and started rifling through the nearest boxes.

"Girls, why don't you go up to your new room and play with your toys?" Jenn suggested. "I've left them in there so you can play for a while. After all, Mummy and Daddy have a lot of unpacking to do."

"OK, Mummy!" the girls chirped before dashing out of the living room and up the stairs.

Angela began looking around the room, carefully manoeuvring around the mountains of boxes. "Oh yes, this is a lovely house – it's so light and airy," she said, before pausing thoughtfully. "Although, there is a lot of energy flowing through it… there's almost a kind of ominous feeling to it, especially in this area," she added, her back to the couple as she inspected the fireplace.

David and Jenn exchanged a glance, David rolling

his eyes and shaking his head ever so slightly, which made Jenn break out into a wide grin. She quickly turned away and pretended to busy herself unpacking boxes to keep from laughing out loud.

"Well, it is an old house, Mum," David pointed out. "I imagine there's been a lot of energy coming and going through it over the years."

Angela turned to face him, her expression serious. David was now stacking boxes in the corner of the room, trying to appear preoccupied. "Hmm," she mused. "Well, next time I visit, I'll bring my sage to burn and cleanse the house for you both. A cleansed house is a happy house!"

David shifted into humouring mode, giving Angela a big, exaggerated smile. "That would be great, Mum, thank you. Now, why don't you go and check on the kids and see what they want for dinner? We were thinking about getting a takeaway tonight since half the kitchen is still packed in these boxes."

"Oh, that's a great idea, son! I fancy a Chinese veggie curry," Angela replied brightly.

"Sure, Mum, whatever you want – it's our treat."

"Fantastic, thank you!" Angela said as she headed upstairs to find the children.

As soon as Angela was out of earshot, Jenn stopped what she was doing and began sniffing the air around her.

David noticed and frowned, confused. "What are you doing?" he asked her.

"Can't you smell that?" Jenn replied, still sniffing.

"Smell what?"

"Cigarette smoke… I can smell cigarette smoke. I

just got a strong whiff of it," Jenn told him, sniffing the air again.

David took a sniff too. "I can't smell anything."

Jenn frowned. "I can definitely smell it, David," she insisted.

David rolled his eyes. "Well, none of us smoke, so it's probably from the previous owners. You must have disturbed some dust that was caked in nicotine or something."

"Hmm," Jenn replied, her tone uncertain, "maybe."

After a few hours spent sorting and unpacking boxes, David set about building the children's bunk beds in their room. It didn't take him long. By now, he was feeling incredibly tired, but it was a happy kind of tired. He was just glad they'd finally moved in.

Meanwhile, Jenn was downstairs organising the kitchen cupboards. The kitchen-diner was open-plan, thanks to the large extension. It certainly made the house feel more spacious. The kitchen itself, however, was old, tired, and dated, though Jenn knew she'd be able to spruce it up a bit until they could afford to buy a brand-new one. *Nothing a bit of cupboard paint can't fix,* she thought.

Earlier in the day, David and Jenn had transported the family pets to the new house in the car. She had placed Thumper, their rabbit, by the far window in the kitchen-diner to let him settle into his new surroundings. Lola, their cat, had been left to roam freely and explore the large back garden and neighbouring areas.

When they first arrived, Jenn had noticed that Thumper seemed agitated and unsettled. He'd been running back and forth in his cage, stamping his feet vigorously. She knew that this kind of behaviour often meant that the rabbit was sensing danger or feeling threatened.

Pausing in her task of stacking tins in the cupboard, Jenn walked over to the cage and knelt down. "Hey, little man, what's up with you?" she asked softly.

Thumper froze in place and looked up at her, his little chest heaving in and out as though he were having a panic attack. Concerned, Jenn opened the cage and tried to pick him up, but he darted around the cage so quickly that she struggled to catch hold of him. When she finally managed to pick him up, Thumper resisted with all his strength, doing everything in his power to wriggle free. He kicked his powerful back legs, scratched Jenn with his claws, and even bit one of her fingers hard enough to draw blood.

"Ouch!" Jenn cried, wincing. "Calm down, Thumper – it's only me! What's wrong with you today?"

The rabbit continued struggling, but she eventually positioned him in the crook of her arm, holding him like a baby – a technique she'd learnt that usually helped relax rabbits. In response, Thumper began to settle slightly, but Jenn could still feel his little heart racing under her hand. She stroked his head and gently rubbed his ears, whispering, "It's OK. There's a good boy. Calm down."

Despite her efforts, Thumper remained agitated, so Jenn decided to put him back. As soon as she lowered him, he wriggled out of her arms, darting into the little house in the corner of his cage.

Jenn sighed, closed the cage, and stood up. As she

walked back to the kitchen, she rubbed her bitten finger, puzzled. He'd never bitten her before. While she resumed putting the tins away, her eyes kept drifting back to the rabbit's cage, her brow furrowed in concern.

Just then, David walked into the kitchen. "Jenn, I've finished rebuilding the kids' bunk beds," he informed her. "I'll build ours in the morning; we can sleep on the mattress tonight."

"OK, honey, that's good," Jenn replied quietly, clearly distracted.

"Are you OK?" he asked, concerned.

Jenn snapped out of her reverie and turned to face him. "Yeah, I'm fine. Thumper is acting really strange, though – he seems very agitated. He keeps running around his cage and stamping his feet. And he bit me!" she added, holding her finger up for him to inspect.

After giving her finger the once-over, David glanced across the room at the rabbit's cage. Thumper had cautiously emerged from his little house and was now looking around. "He's probably just out of sorts, trying to get used to his new surroundings," he suggested. "I'm sure he'll be back to his usual self tomorrow."

"Yeah, you're probably right," Jenn replied, though she still seemed a bit unsure.

David put his arms around Jenn's waist, and she looped hers around his neck. "How about we get the kids to bed and then open that bottle of champagne your mum gave us as a housewarming gift?" he suggested, smiling.

Jenn returned the smile. "And then maybe we can christen our bedroom too?"

David chuckled. "Maybe, if you're lucky… though

I'm not one for putting out after a couple of glasses of champagne – I'm a classy lady!"

Jenn laughed and kissed him on the lips. "Well, in that case, how about I try to find the other bottle of wine I've got stashed somewhere?"

David's smile widened. "Yeah, that would probably do it," he replied.

Chapter 2

The next morning, the kids came bursting through David and Jenn's bedroom door, full of energy.

"Mummy, Daddy!" they both cried as they leapt onto the mattress where David and Jenn were sleeping.

David groaned as he looked at his smartwatch. "It's 6:23 am on a Saturday morning," he sighed, feeling worse for wear and bleary-eyed.

"Yup, that sounds about right – it's like clockwork with these two," Jenn said, chuckling as the kids jumped all over their mum and dad, giggling.

David rubbed his eyes and face, letting out another sigh. "I feel terrible," he told his wife. "It was such a great idea of yours to have the champagne *and* that whole bottle of wine last night."

"I didn't see you saying no to any of it, sweetheart," Jenn pointed out, "and it's not like I forced it down your neck, is it?"

"Daddy, I'm hungry! I want my breakfast," Bella interrupted.

"OK, sweetheart. I think Mummy is going to get it for you," David said with a hopeful glance at Jenn.

"I don't think so!" Jenn scoffed. "It's your turn to get up with them; I got up with them last weekend," she added with a sarcastic smile.

David groaned. "Well, that's great, isn't it? So, you got me drunk last night, had your wicked way with me, and now that I'm terminally hungover, I have to get up with the kids?"

Jenn grinned. "Yup, pretty much."

David inhaled deeply, rubbed his face again, and let out a loud sigh. "OK, come on, kids. Let's go and get some breakfast."

The children squealed with excitement and bolted out of the bedroom, racing down the stairs. David groaned again as he tried to haul himself off the mattress.

He staggered downstairs like a zombie desperately in need of caffeine. Grabbing a coffee pod, he threw it into the machine and switched it on as the kids grew increasingly rowdy, sitting at the table and waiting for their breakfast.

"Right, kids, that's enough. Settle down – it's far too early for all this noise," David said, his tone weary. But the girls clearly weren't listening – instead, they'd started squabbling over something.

As David poured their cereal and milk into two bowls, Olivia began to cry and Bella started shouting.

"She took my toy!" Olivia wailed.

"I had this toy earlier, and now I want it back!" Bella shouted defensively, holding it up in the air.

David let out another loud sigh, gripping the edge of

the counter. "Right, that's enough, you two!" he snapped, his patience wearing thin. He then picked up the two bowls of cereal, placed them on the table in front of the kids, and sat down with a tired sigh. "Bella, you know better than to take things out of your little sister's hands. That's not nice, is it?"

"But, Daddy, I had it first!" Bella protested.

"Then ask her for it, Bella. Don't just snatch it out of her hand." Then, turning to Olivia, David knelt beside her, trying to calm her down.

Olivia, however, wasn't having any of it.

"OK, Olivia," David began, his voice weary but gentle, "Daddy is going to be honest with you. I'm not feeling very well this morning. It's 6.30 am on a Saturday, I haven't had my coffee yet, and I've got a really bad headache. Now, it could be that I'm coming down with a head cold or the flu or something, *or* it could be because of all the wine and champagne Mummy gave me last night. I don't know – I'm not a doctor. But I really need you to calm down and stop crying. Can you do that for me, please?"

Oliva paused her wailing and stared at her dad, as though processing his words. For a brief moment, it seemed like she might stop crying altogether. But then, just as suddenly, she burst into tears again – this time even louder than before.

David groaned again, rubbing his face in frustration. He then stood up and shuffled over to the coffee machine, eager to get his first strong cup of the day. As the machine sputtered to life, he poured his coffee, took a long, deep sip, and closed his eyes in blissful relief.

Meanwhile, Bella had started eating her cereal but was now glancing over at the rabbit cage. "Look!" she exclaimed. "Thumper's still sleeping!"

David took another long, deep slurp of his coffee and exhaled slowly. "Mmm," he muttered, barely registering her words.

"Daddy, look at Thumper!" Bella continued, her tone more insistent this time.

David turned, his attention finally drawn to the rabbit's cage. Thumper was lying in the middle, unusually still. A frown crept across David's face.

Typically, when Thumper heard the kids in the morning, he'd perk up and run to the side of the cage to beg for attention. But not today. Plus, with Olivia crying at the volume of a jumbo jet taking off, it seemed impossible for any living creature to sleep through the racket.

A terrible feeling washed over David as he stared at the cage, his heart sinking.

Bella placed the toy she'd taken from Olivia onto the table, hopped off her chair, and ran over to Thumper's cage. Olivia, who had instantly stopped crying upon seeing the unattended toy, grabbed it from the table and followed her big sister.

David sighed, set his coffee down, and walked over to the cage as well.

"Come on, Thumper… wake up, sleepyhead!" Bella said, tapping the cage lightly.

Olivia giggled. "Sleepy wabbit!"

The moment David looked at Thumper, he knew. The rabbit's lifeless body was stiff, the tell-tale sign that rigor mortis had set in hours ago. Even so, he tried to remain composed as the kids continued tapping the cage, utterly oblivious. "Right, kids – come on. Leave him alone," David said gently. "It's his weekend too; he just wants a lie-in, like Mummy. Go finish your cereal, and Daddy will put the TV on for you."

The kids, apparently satisfied with this explanation, skipped back to the table to finish their breakfast.

David didn't have the heart to tell them the truth – not now, not while he was still hungover and struggling to keep his own emotions in check. So, instead, he grabbed a throw blanket from the couch and draped it carefully over the cage.

Jenn can deal with the emotional carnage later, he thought grimly.

At 10:36 am, David decided it was time to wake Jenn. He made her a coffee – strong, with milk and one sugar, just the way she liked it – and carried it upstairs. "Jenn, it's time to wake up," he said softly, nudging her shoulder.

"What time is it?" she mumbled groggily, rubbing her eyes.

"It's nearly 11 am," David replied sheepishly.

Jenn sat up, resting her back against the wall as David handed her the coffee. "Are the kids OK?" she asked.

David hesitated for a moment, then nodded. "Yeah, they're fine," he replied. "They're playing on their iPads." He exhaled deeply, running a hand through his hair. "Look, Jenn, there's no easy way to say this, so I'll just come out with it… the rabbit's dead. It looks like he passed away during the night."

Jenn didn't know whether to laugh or cry. David had a very dark and very dry sense of humour, and sometimes it was hard to tell if he was joking or being serious. This time, however, she could tell just by looking at his face. "How did he... what happened?" she asked hesitantly.

"I don't know, sweetheart. I haven't had a chance to look at him properly," he explained. "The kids noticed he was lying down and they thought he was sleeping. I took one look at him and knew he was gone, so I put one of the couch throws over his cage and told the kids he was having a lie-in."

Jenn's eyes started to well up. "Maybe it was the shock of the move that killed him," she said, tears spilling down her cheeks. She placed her coffee mug on the floor beside the mattress and wiped her face with trembling hands.

David pulled her into a hug as she sobbed quietly. He held her for a few moments, rubbing her back and letting her cry.

Eventually, Jenn composed herself, took a deep breath, and went downstairs. She immediately made a fuss of the kids, kissing their cheeks and smoothing their hair.

David followed closely behind her. "OK, girls," he said, crouching to their level. "Why don't you go upstairs, brush your teeth, and wash your faces? Daddy will come up in a minute to help you get dressed."

"OK, Daddy!" they chirped, setting their iPads down on the couch and running upstairs to the bathroom.

Once the kids were out of sight, David and Jenn walked over to Thumper's cage. Jenn hesitated before slowly pulling the throw off the top, and then David unclipped the side of the cage, opening it carefully. He reached in and gently picked up the rabbit's lifeless body. It was stiff as a board, but its head hung limp.

David looked up at Jenn, his face pale. "It looks like…"

"Like what?" Jenn asked, frowning.

"Like his neck has been broken," he said quietly.

Jenn raised a hand to her mouth, letting out a gasp as tears streamed down her face again, the weight of the situation hitting her in an instant. "Oh my God!" she cried. "How the hell did he break his neck?"

David shrugged. "My guess is he snapped it, running back and forth in his cage… maybe he hit his head a bit too hard."

Jenn started sobbing again. "He was so unsettled last night; I should have kept a closer eye on him," she told her husband, her voice trembling.

David gently placed Thumper back in the cage, stood up, and wrapped his arms around his wife. "You can't blame yourself, Jenn. There's no way you could have known this would happen. It was probably just the stress of the move and his new surroundings that made him so unsettled."

Jenn wiped the tears from her face. "I know," she said softly. "I just feel so guilty… and I have no idea what we're going to tell the kids."

David placed a comforting hand on her shoulder. "We'll just tell them the truth – that he fell asleep and went to Heaven," he said with a reassuring smile. "Now, come on – we can do this. I'll go upstairs, get the kids ready, and take a quick shower while you have a few moments to calm down and pull yourself together. Then we'll sit them down, explain what happened, and let them pick a nice spot in the garden to bury him."

Jenn just about managed a weak smile, nodding gently.

So, later that morning, David and Jenn gathered the kids in the living room to explain what had happened. They told them that Thumper had gone to sleep and, sadly, never woke up.

As expected, the children didn't take the news well. It was their first experience with death, and they struggled to comprehend how their beloved rabbit could just be gone.

After they'd calmed down, David took them outside to choose a spot to bury Thumper. They picked a quiet corner of the garden, shaded by a tree.

David dug a small hole while Jenn suggested they decorate an old shoebox to lay Thumper in before burying him. The children liked the idea and got busy drawing and colouring on the box, turning it into a special resting place for their pet. The act of decorating the shoebox – and placing Thumper's favourite toys inside – seemed to help the girls come to terms with their loss.

Once they were finished, David gently placed the rabbit inside the box, next to its toys, and together they took him out into the garden for the burial.

David suggested getting a small plaque made up with Thumper's name on it to attach to the fence near his resting place. "That way, you can visit him every day," he told the girls, which seemed to bring them a little comfort.

Though it was a sad day, Jenn couldn't help but reflect on how important it was as a life lesson for the kids to come to terms with death; while it was painful, it was also a chance for them to learn about loss and love.

The Black Finger Man

***

Later that afternoon, David noticed something odd – Lola, their two-year-old tabby cat, hadn't set foot inside the house since the move.

David and Jenn had adopted Lola when she was a tiny seven-week-old kitten, and she had quickly become the heart of their home.

The inspiration for her name came from one of David and Jenn's favourite rock bands, the Danish group Volbeat. One of their most successful singles, 'Lola Montez,' was a tribute to the famous stage dancer. From the moment they brought the little cat home, her name was destined to be Lola.

Jenn was upstairs, pottering around in the bedrooms and organising the remaining boxes.

"Jenn!" David called upstairs. "Have you seen Lola? I haven't seen her since we moved in!"

"No, I haven't," Jenn called back. "Why don't you shake her box of treats? She's probably out exploring!"

So, David went to the cupboard, grabbed the small Tupperware box of Lola's treats, and stepped out the back door. Shaking the box, he called out into the garden, "Lola! Lola! Come and get a biscuit!"

David stopped shaking the box for a moment, scanning the garden carefully and listening for any sign of the cat. He couldn't see or hear her at all.

His worry began to grow. He remembered watching countless nature documentaries that warned of cats becoming disoriented during a house move. Often, they tried to find their way back to their old home, no matter how far away it was.

He shook the box again, more urgently this time. "Lola! Lola! Come on, darling… come and get a biscuit!"

Just as his anxiety was building, he noticed movement at the far end of the garden – the bottom of the hedge was rustling and shaking. A moment later, Lola popped her head out from under the hedge and bounded towards him.

Relief flooded through David, and he broke into a broad smile. Dropping to one knee, he made a massive fuss of her. "Hello, my darling! Where have you been? Have you been out exploring? We missed you!"

Lola rubbed herself around his legs, purring loudly as David stroked her.

"Come on then, puss," he said warmly. "Come and get a biscuit."

He let her into the house and placed a few biscuits in her bowl, watching as she eagerly crunched on them. She seemed fine.

Later that night, however, Lola started to act very strangely. She couldn't settle, pacing around the house with her fur sticking up and her tail fluffed out – a clear sign that she was on high alert and felt threatened.

As she darted past him, David managed to scoop her up. "Lola, calm down, it's OK," he murmured, holding her close.

Lola was clearly distressed, wriggling and struggling in David's arms as he tried to calm her. It was no use – her ears were pinned back, her pupils were fully dilated, and her eyes darted wildly in every direction. Her breathing was rapid and shallow.

Suddenly, she extended her claws into David's arms

in a frantic attempt to escape. "Ouch!" he yelped, jerking in pain as she climbed over his right shoulder and jumped onto the floor. Without hesitation, the cat bolted up the stairs.

"Lola! What the hell is wrong with you tonight?" David shouted after her, exasperated.

He looked down at his arm and saw several red, angry scratches where her claws had broken the skin. With a sigh, he walked to the kitchen cupboard, opened it, and rummaged through the first aid kit for the Germolene ointment.

At that moment, Jenn came into the kitchen, her brow furrowed. "What's all the shouting about? What happened?"

David turned to face her, holding up his scratched arm. "That silly cat! I picked her up for a cuddle to try and calm her down, and she scratched me to bits. Look!"

Jenn gasped, her eyes widening at the sight of his arm. "Oh my God! She's never done that before… she's probably just unsettled because of the move. Like poor Thumper."

David nodded in agreement as he applied the ointment. "I know she didn't mean it. She's obviously just not used to the house yet. I'll grab her some catnip treats tomorrow on my way home from work. Hopefully, that'll settle her."

***

Unfortunately, Lola didn't settle at all when David and Jenn went to bed that night. She ran all over the house, shrieking and hissing. Needless to say, David and Jenn got very little sleep.

By 6 am, Lola was scratching and yowling at the back door to be let out. David trudged downstairs with the kids, bleary-eyed, to make coffee for himself and Jenn, along with breakfast for the children.

By this point, Lola's scratching and meowing had reached a fever pitch. David sighed heavily as he made his way from the kitchen to the back door. "Alright, alright, I'm coming, Lola. Calm down – I'll let you out," he muttered, still groggy.

He opened the back door, and Lola shot outside as fast as a bullet. Darting to the end of the garden, she disappeared under the hedge.

"Silly cat," David muttered, rolling his eyes before heading back to the kitchen.

Later that morning, as David and Jenn were getting the kids ready to load into the car for school and nursery, Bella suddenly shouted from the back living room window.

"Look!" she cried. "There's another cat in the garden with Lola!"

Olivia ran up to the window, pressing her face against the glass for a better look.

Sure enough, there was another cat in the garden – a sleek black cat with piercing green eyes. Lola's fur was bristling, her tail puffed up like a bottlebrush. Her back was arched as she slowly circled the black cat, trying to make herself appear larger.

Olivia giggled. "Lola made a friend!" she exclaimed.

David stepped up to the window and took in the scene. The black cat was now circling Lola, its fur raised and tail fluffed out just like hers. The two cats moved in tense, deliberate steps, their eyes locked on each other. *Looks more like a good old-fashioned cat turf war,* David thought, watching the stand-off.

Just then, the cats began to fight viciously, screeching and screaming as they rolled across the grass, swiping and kicking at each other with sharp claws.

Bella's eyes filled with tears. "Oh no! Daddy, do something! Lola's going to get hurt!"

David knelt down beside her, placing a comforting hand on her shoulder. "Darling, I can't do anything. Lola's a cat and this garden is her territory now. It probably used to be the black cat's territory because the house was empty for so long. Now, Lola has to make it hers. Remember the nature programmes you watched with Daddy?"

Bella nodded.

"Well, this is the same thing," he told her with a small smile. "It's just nature – it's what cats do. They fight all the time."

"But I don't want her to get hurt," Bella said softly, her lower lip trembling.

David smiled reassuringly. "I know you don't, darling. And she won't get hurt; Lola knows what she's doing."

Bella looked up at her dad with sad, worried eyes.

David sighed, stood up, and tapped loudly on the window, the sharp sound instantly breaking up the fight. Both cats froze, looking around to locate the noise.

The black cat hissed, clearly spooked, and bolted under the hedge, disappearing from sight. Lola stood her ground, watching to ensure the intruder was truly gone before she began vigorously grooming herself.

"See?" David said, smiling as he gestured to Lola. "She knows what she's doing. Now, come on – we're going to be late."

***

During the workweek, David and Jenn had a usual routine. After putting the kids to bed at around 7 pm, they would stay upstairs, snuggle up in their bedroom, and watch TV until around 9:30 pm. They aimed to be asleep by 10 pm, ready to wake up at 6:30 am the next morning.

David typically took a little longer to fall asleep, but lately, his work caseload had been more demanding than usual. He was so exhausted that, on this particular night, he was fast asleep and snoring within minutes.

Jenn, however, wasn't so lucky. As much as she loved David, his snoring was incredibly loud – loud enough to make falling asleep nearly impossible.

Frustrated, she picked up her phone to check the time – it was 11:59 pm. She let out a heavy sigh, set the phone back down, and put her head back on her pillow, staring up at the ceiling. For two hours she lay there, listening to the relentless sound of David's snoring.

Finally, David rolled onto his side and the snoring subsided. Jenn breathed a sigh of relief, closed her eyes, and began to gently drift off.

Suddenly, the bedroom door rattled as if someone were trying to open it.

Jenn gasped, her body going rigid with fear as her stomach churned. She was wide awake now, adrenaline coursing through her veins. She grabbed her phone again, activating the torch. The screen showed that it was 12 am exactly. Bang on midnight.

Heart pounding, she got out of bed and crept to the bedroom door. Her hand trembled as she placed it on the handle. Then, with a quick motion, she flung the door open, holding her breath.

There was no one there.

Confused, Jenn stepped into the hallway, her phone's light guiding her. She crept to the kids' room and slowly opened their door. Both children were sleeping soundly, their breathing soft and even.

What the hell was that? she thought, her mind racing.

She tried to calm herself down as she walked back into her bedroom, closing the door behind her. Looking over at David, she saw him curled up in the foetal position, snoring softly. He looked so peaceful – even a little cute.

But I could still wring his neck for keeping me awake with his snoring, she thought wryly as she climbed back into bed.

Chapter 3

A few months later, the family had settled into their new house. David and Jenn still had a lot of decorating to do, but they were tackling it bit by bit – usually at weekends and occasionally in the evenings during the week, depending on their energy levels.

David had tidied up the garden as best he could. He mowed the lawn, strimmed the edges, and cleared away years of accumulated junk and rubbish.

Ideally, David and Jenn would have the whole thing landscaped. However, they decided to prioritise the inside of the house and revisit the garden project next year.

One Saturday afternoon, they received a cheap plastic Wendy house and a basic swing set that Jenn had ordered from Amazon. David assembled them that same day, and the girls absolutely loved them. The garden was starting to feel like a fun, welcoming space for the kids, and the house itself was beginning to feel like a home.

On this warm spring day, David was decluttering and reorganising the garage to create more storage space, while Jenn focused on her usual cleaning and tidying inside. The children played happily in the back garden, their laughter drifting through the open windows.

Jenn glanced out to check on them and noticed they weren't alone; they were playing with a little boy who looked to be around the same age as Bella. He had dark brown hair styled in a bowl cut and wore a T-shirt and shorts.

Jenn assumed he was from next door and had popped through the gap in the fence. She didn't mind – in fact, she was glad the girls had made a new friend.

David walked in from the garage, covered in dust and wiping his hands on his jeans. He went straight to the kitchen sink to wash them. "The garage looks a lot better now," he said. "I threw out loads of crap that had been left in there. I've loaded up the car to take the rest of it to the tip."

Jenn nodded. "Great!"

"Who's the little boy playing with the girls?" David asked, glancing out into the garden.

Jenn turned to him with a smile. "I don't know – he just appeared. I think he lives next door."

David nodded, smiling. "Well, whoever he is, at least the kids have made a little friend."

"That's what I thought," Jenn replied, tapping on the window and waving.

All three of the kids looked up, smiled brightly, and waved back.

***

Jenn had just finished in the bathroom and was washing her hands in the basin when a cold shiver ran down her spine. Out of the corner of her eye, she thought she saw something move. She gasped, her heart skipping a beat.

Quickly, she turned to look, but the bathroom was empty. Of course, no one was there.

She dried her hands hastily and moved to leave, but as she tried to close the door behind her, she felt resistance – like some unseen force was pulling against it from the other side. Startled, Jenn grabbed the handle with both hands and pulled with all her strength, trying to shut the door completely.

Her breath quickened. *What is going on?* she thought.

After a moment, she let go of the handle and took a step back. Then, just as she turned to walk away, the bathroom door began to rattle violently, the handle shaking as though someone were on the other side trying to get out.

Jenn froze, a chill sweeping over her as she stared at the door. A couple of seconds later, the rattling stopped abruptly, leaving the room eerily silent.

A strange, unsettling feeling came over her, then – she felt like she was being watched.

Without another moment's hesitation, she hurried back down the stairs, her pulse racing.

Later that day, Jenn recounted the experience to David. He listened to her story, but then waved it off with a dismissive shrug. "It was probably just the wind or something," he said, before carrying on with his chores.

***

It was 3.15 pm and David had just come in from work. He headed straight to the kitchen and put the kettle on to make himself a cup of tea. He still had notes to write up before it was time to collect the kids from after school care and nursery.

Deciding to get comfortable, he went upstairs to change out of his work uniform. Once he'd slipped into his tracksuit bottoms and a fresh T-shirt, he left the bedroom, closed the door, and tossed his work polo shirt into the dirty laundry basket on the landing.

As he walked past the kids' room on his way downstairs, he didn't notice the figure sitting on Olivia's bottom bunk bed. It was a young girl with long, dark hair, wearing what appeared to be a white dress or gown. She held one of the children's dolls in her hands and silently watched as David walked by.

David had just descended the first two steps when he heard a noise behind him, apparently coming from the kids' room – a soft *thud*, like something falling to the floor. He frowned and stopped in his tracks. Then, turning around, he walked back up the two steps and popped his head around the kids' bedroom doorframe.

The figure was gone. There was no sign of the girl who'd been sitting on the bed.

David's eyes scanned the room until he spotted the doll lying on the floor near the bottom bunk. He walked in, picked it up, and studied it for a moment. It felt cold in his hands. He shrugged, assuming it had simply fallen off the bed.

David placed the doll back on the bed and left the room, heading downstairs to make his tea and finish writing up his notes.

***

The family was sitting around the table, eating dinner, when Jenn turned to the kids. "So, what's your little friend's name, girls? It looked like you were all having great fun the other day in the garden."

Olivia shrugged and continued eating her dinner. Bella mumbled something, her mouth full of food.

"Bella, please don't talk with your mouth full," David told her.

Bella rolled her eyes but began chewing with her mouth closed. After swallowing, she replied, "His name is Andy."

Jenn smiled. "That's nice. Does he live next door?"

This time Bella shrugged. "I don't know."

Jenn and David exchanged a glance as David cleared his throat. "Well, didn't you ask? That's usually what you do when you meet someone – especially if they're in your garden! You say, 'What's your name? Where do you live? How old are you? What school do you go to?'"

Bella looked up at her dad, exasperated. "He's six, and his name is Andy. I don't know where he lives or what school he goes to," she said, rolling her eyes dramatically again.

Jenn tried to hide her smile, as did David.

"OK, Bella the teenager," David teased, leaning over to tickle her.

Bella burst into giggles, squirming in her chair as he continued.

"Maybe next time you see him, you can ask where he lives," David suggested. "Then Mummy and Daddy can get to know his mummy and daddy, too."

"I'll ask him next time, Daddy!" Olivia said excitedly.

David and Jenn both smiled.

"That's great, Olivia," David said. "Now, eat your dinner and I'll see what we can have for pudding."

***

Jenn came in from work, her tough day written all over her face. She wasn't in the best of moods as she stepped into the hallway to take off her shoes, and her eyes immediately landed on one of the family portrait pictures, which was tilted awkwardly to the left. With a tut and a sigh, she straightened it before heading further into the house.

In the kitchen, David was sitting at the table, typing up his patient notes on his laptop. Dinner was gently simmering on the hob, the aroma filling the room. He had picked up the kids from after school care and nursery a few hours earlier and had started preparing the evening meal a little while ago.

Jenn walked into the kitchen, glanced around, and sighed heavily at the chaos spilling into the living room. Toys and colouring books were scattered everywhere, as though the kids had emptied every shelf and drawer they could reach.

David looked up from his laptop, his face lighting up when he saw her. "Hey, babe. How was your day?" he asked warmly.

"Terrible, David! And it's got a hell of a lot worse since I stepped through the door!" Jenn snapped.

David's smile quickly disappeared, replaced by a look of confusion. "Why? What's up?"

"What's up? *Look* at this place! By the looks of things, you've let the kids run amok in here!"

"They were only playing, Jenn. Calm down," he said defensively.

"Calm down?! It'll take a bottle of gin for me to calm down at this rate! I'm fed up with this, David. Every night I come home from work to a house that's a complete state, and I'm the one who has to clean it up! Do you all think I'm just here to clean up after everyone? Well, I'm not!" she bellowed.

David sighed, took off his glasses, and rubbed his eyes. Then, without a word, he stood up and walked over to the kitchen door. "Kids!" he shouted up the stairs. "Come down and tidy up the living room like I told you to do 15 minutes ago!"

Jenn started picking up toys from the floor and tossing them into the toy box with sharp movements. David walked back into the living area and silently joined her.

"I don't understand how you're completely oblivious when they start pulling things out and making a mess, David!" Jenn snapped, her frustration boiling over.

"I was typing up my notes, Jenn," David said, his tone calm but weary. "I saw five patients today, and they were all complicated cases. You know what the job's like. I mean, yeah, it's a bit of an inconvenience that the place is untidy, but at least the kids were playing nicely for a change. Plus, I made dinner when I got in – it's on the hob. It just needs to be dished up."

Jenn crossed her arms. "Yeah, and that's another thing I'll have to do!" she spat back. "And you'd better tell your mum to stop messing about with our pictures!

She might like skewed pictures and mirrors in her house, but I don't like them in mine!"

David frowned, looking even more confused than ever. "What are you talking about? My mum hasn't been here today."

Jenn scoffed. "Well, I just walked in, and the picture in the hallway was squint. I *just* straightened it!" she snapped.

David sighed and rolled his eyes. "OK, no problem. I'll tell her," he said, heading to the hob to start dishing up dinner. As he plated the food, the kids came downstairs and began tidying up the living room as instructed.

Jenn, still fuming, suddenly began coughing. She covered her mouth, frantically searching her work bag for her asthma inhaler. After a moment of digging, she found it, brought it to her lips, and inhaled deeply. The coughing subsided as she worked to steady her breathing.

David put down the ladle and walked over to her, placing a reassuring hand on her shoulder. "That cough is getting worse, Jenn. I really think you need to get it checked out."

Jenn turned to him, her eyes heavy with guilt. "I know it is. I've been putting it off, but I'll make an appointment tomorrow morning."

David pulled her into a gentle hug, wrapping his arms around her as she buried her face in his chest with a long sigh.

"I'm sorry," she said softly. "I came through the door a right grumpy bitch. I've just had a horrible day, and I'm worried about this cough. I took it out on you, and you didn't deserve that."

David cupped Jenn's face in his hand and smiled. "It's OK, don't worry about it," he replied, his tone gentle. "I can be like the Hulk on steroids at times. We all have tough days."

This made Jenn smile.

"But let's not stress about the cough," David continued. "Let's just get it checked out first. Worrying about it isn't going to help, is it?"

Jenn sighed, nodding. "Yeah, you're right."

David grinned. "Of course I'm right. A wise guy is always right. Even when he's wrong, he's right!"

As usual, Jenn laughed at David's terrible Al Pacino impression, her mood lifting a little. She giggled and tapped his chest. "You're such a doofus sometimes."

David's grin widened. "I know. That's one of the reasons you married me, remember?"

The next day, Jenn called the doctor's surgery to arrange an appointment, managing to book a slot for later in the following week.

***

Mother's Day was fast approaching, and David had thought of the perfect gift for Jenn from the kids; he decided to create a collage of all her favourite family photos. So, he scoured his phone for pictures of Jenn with the kids, as well as photos of the four of them that Jenn had sent him over the years. Then, using an app on his phone, he carefully arranged the collage and sent it to an online company to be turned into a print.

It arrived a few days before Mother's Day, and David hid it out of sight.

On the special day, he and the kids woke Jenn up with breakfast in bed and Mother's Day cards. Bella had made her own card for her mummy, and Olivia proudly presented the one she'd made at nursery. They showered Jenn with love and attention before giving her the print.

Jenn's face lit up when she saw it. "I absolutely love it!" she exclaimed, holding it close. She looked at David with a warm smile. "Can you hang it above the TV, here in our bedroom? I'd love to wake up and see it every morning."

David nodded and went to fetch his hammer and a nail. Jenn stood nearby, directing him precisely where to hang it – her perfectionism shining through. Or, as David thought of it, her tendency to be anal-retentive. He followed her instructions to the letter and stepped back when it was done.

"Perfect!" Jenn declared with a big smile. "That is the best present I've ever had!"

They spent the rest of the day enjoying some quality family time together. They went to the park, got ice cream, and later dined at Jenn's favourite restaurant. The perfect end to a perfect day.

The following day, Jenn attended her doctor's appointment.

After examining her chest and lungs, the doctor seemed a little concerned and decided to make a referral to radiology for an X-ray.

***

One evening, David and Jenn were putting the kids to bed. The girls had brushed their teeth and climbed into their bunk beds – Bella, being the oldest, on the top bunk, and Olivia on the bottom. As part of their nightly routine, David left the landing light on and opened the kids' bedroom door wide to let the light flood in while they said goodnight.

This served two purposes: first, to signal to the girls that it was time to settle down, and second, because David had unscrewed and removed the light bulb from their room. Bella had a tendency to egg on her little sister, getting her to turn the light back on and cause chaos at bedtime, so this was his way of avoiding any nighttime antics.

The routine was simple. David would kiss and say goodnight to one of the girls while Jenn tucked in the other, then they would swap before leaving the room.

On this particular night, David was standing beside Bella's bed on the top bunk, tucking her in and giving her a goodnight kiss. Jenn was crouched down at Olivia's bed, doing the same. As they swapped, with David bending down to Olivia and Jenn standing up from the bottom bunk, they both froze.

A shadow moved across the doorway, briefly blocking the light from the landing, then disappeared as if someone had just walked past.

Oliva gasped. "What was that?" she whispered, her voice trembling.

David and Jenn exchanged a startled look, cold shivers running down their spines.

David knew he had to stay calm and play this down. The last thing he wanted was to upset the kids – or worse, Jenn – just before bedtime. He was well aware that if

Jenn got even a hint of something unusual, she would run with it and he'd never hear the end of her superstitions and conspiracy theories. He'd been hoping for a peaceful evening in front of the TV to watch the football.

"It was probably just a power surge," David said casually. "This is an old house, and it needs rewiring. Stuff like this happens all the time in old buildings."

"No! I saw something move across the door!" Bella cried, her eyes wide with fear.

Jenn gave David a worried look.

He sighed, walking over to the door and peering onto the landing. "See? There's nothing out here," he said, stepping aside to show them. Then, he walked back over to the bunk beds and smiled reassuringly. "It's just an old house, nothing to worry about. Now, lie down and go to sleep, you two."

"OK, Daddy. Goodnight," said Bella.

"Love you," added Olivia.

"I love you both too. Goodnight," David said, kissing their foreheads before stepping out of the room.

After Jenn gave Bella a kiss goodnight, she and David walked out onto the landing.

David had recently installed two baby gates – one across the kids' bedroom door and the other at the top of the stairs. As David headed downstairs to the living room, Jenn lingered, slowly closing the kids' bedroom door behind her and securing the baby gate. A worried look clouded her face as she made her way downstairs.

David settled onto the couch, picked up the remote, and turned on the TV. He planned to watch the football while Jenn watched one of her chick flicks upstairs in the bedroom.

But instead of heading upstairs, Jenn walked into the living room and sat on the opposite couch, her expression troubled. "Don't you think that was weird, David?" she asked.

David glanced away from the TV, raising an eyebrow. "What? A power surge? Nothing weird about that, sweetheart." He shrugged. "Like I said, it's just an old house."

Jenn shook her head, unconvinced. "I don't know, David… that didn't seem like a power surge to me. That seemed like a shadow."

"A shadow? Of what? Or who?" David asked, leaning back on the couch. "We're the only ones in the house, so who could it have been? A ghost?" He chuckled lightly.

Jenn didn't smile. "Well, I don't know. You said it yourself – it's an old house. Just think how many people have lived and probably *died* here."

David rolled his eyes and let out a sigh. "Jenn, you know I don't believe in all that supernatural stuff. Yes, it's an old house, and yes, the electrics need upgrading. The place hasn't been rewired since the 1980s. Why do you think we got it so cheap?"

"Well, I believe in it!" Jenn snapped. "All that 'supernatural stuff,' as you call it. I had a feeling we were being watched, and then I got a cold shiver down my spine."

David sighed heavily, rubbing his eyes before turning to Jenn. "You're starting to sound like my mum, Jenn. Honestly, I should have just married her years ago," he said with a grin.

Jenn frowned. "You're a sarcastic shit at times, do you know that?"

David chuckled, clearly amused.

"Well, David," Jenn continued, "your mum would probably believe me. I *felt* something walk past that door upstairs."

David smirked. "Oh, I don't doubt she'd believe you. In fact, she'd probably insist on coming around to sage the entire house and perform some sort of voodoo ritual whilst singing 'Kumbaya.'"

He laughed again, clearly trying to lighten the mood, but Jenn simply stared at him, unimpressed.

As his laughter faded, Jenn's expression slowly softened. A sly smile spread across her face as she stood up and walked towards the door.

"You know what, David? That's a great idea," she said. "I'll call her right now and ask her to come around tomorrow evening so she can sage the house. Maybe she can bring a few of her hippy mates, and we'll make a night of it. We can all get involved." She left the room with a big smile, closing the door behind her.

David's face dropped, his grin vanishing instantly. "Ah, come on, Jenn! Don't do that – I'm sorry! I was only joking!" he called, quickly getting up and following her out of the room.

***

Later that night, Jenn found herself struggling to sleep again. However, this time, it wasn't due to David's snoring. She couldn't shake the feeling that there was some kind of presence in the house. Her mind kept circling back to the shadow that had walked past the door earlier that evening.

No matter how much she tried, she couldn't convince herself it was just her imagination.

She picked up her phone to check the time. It was 11:59 pm. Her eyes lingered on the digital clock in the top right corner of the screen, watching as the numbers changed to 12 am.

And then, she heard it.

The bedroom door handle rattled violently for a moment, then stopped abruptly.

Jenn's heart raced, though she wasn't as freaked out as she had been the first time it happened. The door handle had been rattling every night at the exact same time since she'd first heard it. By now, she had come to accept it – though it didn't make the experience any less unsettling.

She was convinced they were being visited by some kind of presence – no matter how much David would try to dismiss it and find some kind of 'reasonable explanation.'

There was nothing reasonable about it.

Chapter 4

Before they knew it, another week had slipped by, and it was early Sunday morning. It was David's turn for a lie-in, so Jenn got up with the kids.

She had just made herself a coffee from the machine and was now fixing the kids' breakfast. They wanted cereal, so she grabbed two bowls from the cupboard and filled them with their favourite, Cheerios. After putting the box back in the cupboard, she went to the cutlery drawer, took out two spoons, and placed one in each bowl. Next, she opened the fridge, poured milk over the cereal, returned the carton to the fridge, and carried the bowls to the table, setting them at each child's place.

"Come on, kids – iPads down. Come and get your breakfast."

"OK, Mummy," they replied in unison, setting their devices down and skipping over to the table.

Jenn had her back turned to the rest of the kitchen, focusing on tidying up, when she heard the kids gasp behind her. She turned around, alarmed.

Olivia pulled her big sister closer to her, whimpering. Bella, looking equally frightened, began to whine.

"Girls, what's wrong?" she asked, her face clouded with confusion.

Olivia was now half hiding behind Bella, who was holding her tightly.

Bella raised a trembling hand and pointed towards the kitchen. "Mummy... look," she whispered, her voice breaking.

As Jenn spun around, her breath caught in her throat, her blood running cold.

Every kitchen cupboard door and drawer was wide open.

Jenn took a step back, trying to make sense of what she was seeing.

Was she going mad? Had she opened all the drawers and doors without realising? No, that couldn't be it. Everyone in the house knew that leaving doors and drawers open was Jenn's ultimate pet hate.

The kids started crying, their fear palpable. So, Jenn swallowed her own panic and forced a big smile on her face as she turned back to them. She knew she had to stay calm for their sake.

"What are you two crying for?" she said brightly. "Silly Mummy just forgot to close the doors when I was getting your cereal and bowls."

Bella shook her head, her wide eyes filled with worry. "But Mummy, they were shut when you brought our breakfast in," she said softly.

"No, darling, Mummy just forgot," she insisted. "She hasn't had her coffee yet – she's still sleepy," Jenn replied with a big, reassuring smile. "Why don't you eat your breakfast, and we'll figure out what to do today when Daddy wakes up?"

"OK, Mummy," Bella said.

As the girls settled at the table and began eating their breakfast, Jenn slipped her phone out of her dressing gown pocket and snapped a picture of all the open kitchen drawers and cupboards. As she stared at the image on her screen, a cold tingle ran down her spine. That same disconcerting feeling crept over her again, making her shiver.

Later that morning, when David got up, Jenn showed him the photo. She explained what had happened, her voice tinged with worry.

Once again, however, David dismissed what Jenn was telling him, assuring her that there was a completely reasonable explanation. "It was probably just the kids messing around," he said flippantly.

***

At 2:08 am, in the early hours of Monday morning, a loud crash jolted David and Jenn awake, followed by the sound of shattering glass coming from downstairs.

David jumped out of bed and grabbed the baseball bat he kept hidden at the top of the wardrobe. "Stay up here with the kids, Jenn!" he whispered sternly.

Jenn nodded, clutching the duvet to her as David quietly opened the baby gate at the top of the stairs. He then crept down the staircase, every step deliberate and cautious.

The house was now eerily silent.

David pushed open the living room door, which

creaked slightly as he entered. The room was bathed in an orange glow from the streetlamp outside. Shadows flickered across the walls, but everything seemed still.

He scanned the room, casting an eye towards the windows. He fully expected at least one of them to be broken, but they were all intact.

Frowning, he took another step into the room, hissing in pain as something sharp jabbed into his foot.

"Ouch!" David cried, stepping back and flipping on the light.

The floor was littered with broken glass from what looked like picture frames.

David looked up at the floating shelves near the fireplace, where the frames had once stood, and gasped.

All of the photographs that had been inside the frames were now neatly lined up along the shelf.

David frowned, his confusion deepening. These weren't standard picture frames where you could unclip the backing to insert the photos. Jenn had bought fancy ones online – solidly designed with a small gap at the bottom where you had to carefully slide the photos in.

It didn't make sense; if the frames had fallen, the photos would still be stuck inside, or scattered across the floor along with the millions of pieces of broken glass. But here they were, perfectly arranged on the shelf, as if they'd been placed deliberately.

As he stood there, trying to piece everything together, Jenn crept down the stairs and stepped into the living room.

"Oh my God, what happened here?" she asked, her eyes widening at the mess.

David turned to her, his voice low but steady. "Be careful – there's broken glass everywhere. I've just stepped on some. It looks like the frames fell off the shelf." He gestured towards the floor. "Can you get me the dustpan and brush from under the sink please, sweetheart?"

Jenn nodded. "Yeah… that's really weird, how all the frames fell like that."

David shrugged, trying to dismiss the unease crawling up his spine. "I know. Maybe there's a draught in here that blew them off the shelf. Anyway, just get me the dustpan. I'll sweep this up – you go on back to bed."

"OK. I'll order more frames in the morning," Jenn said as she walked into the kitchen to retrieve the dustpan and brush. She returned a moment later and handed them to David.

"Are the kids OK?" he asked.

"Yeah, they're out cold. They didn't hear a thing," Jenn replied.

David smiled. "They both take after you – you three could sleep through an earthquake," he teased.

Jenn giggled softly as she turned and made her way back upstairs.

David let out a quiet sigh of relief. He was glad she hadn't noticed the pictures still neatly sitting on the shelf. That would have freaked her out completely, and he would never hear the end of it.

***

One evening, Jenn arrived home from work just as the next-door neighbours were pulling into their driveway.

Since moving in, she and David hadn't had the

chance to properly meet the neighbours. Between the chaos of the move, working full time, and dealing with the kids – not to mention the fact that it was the middle of winter when they first moved in– there just hadn't been time. They exchanged friendly smiles and waves whenever they saw each other in passing, but that had been it.

So, as Jenn walked up the driveway, she decided it was the perfect opportunity to officially introduce herself.

With a big smile, she walked up to the fence that separated their properties as the couple got out of their car. "Hi there!" she said cheerily. "I'm Jenn – it's nice to finally meet you!"

"Hi Jenn!" the couple replied in unison.

"I'm Brian, and this is my wife, Linda," the man said, gesturing towards his partner.

Jenn quickly took in their friendly demeanour. Brian was tall and slender, with short grey hair, while Linda was shorter, with shoulder-length blonde hair. Both looked to be in their fifties.

"Have you all settled in OK since the move?" Linda asked.

"Yeah, we're all settled in," Jenn replied. "We're slowly getting there with the decorating now. It's always daunting when you move in and have so much to do, isn't it?"

"Oh, absolutely," Linda agreed. "Mind you, I've always just left it all to Brian. I tell him what I want, and he cracks on with the work!" She chuckled, her laugh sharp but good-natured.

"It's true," Brian said with a grin. "Happy wife, happy life."

Jenn laughed.

"Is your husband handy when it comes to decorating and DIY, Jenn?" Brian asked.

Jenn nodded. "Yeah, David's not too bad when he puts his mind to it. It takes a bit of nagging, but he gets it done eventually," she said with a grin.

They all shared a chuckle.

"And what are your girls' names, Jenn?" Linda asked. "We've seen them playing in the garden."

"Bella and Olivia," Jenn replied. "Bella's the oldest – she rules the roost." She smiled warmly. "And how old is your boy? Andy, isn't it? We see him playing with the girls in our garden sometimes, but I haven't had the chance to meet him yet."

Brian and Linda exchanged a confused look.

"We've got a boy and a girl," Brian said slowly, "but they're both in their twenties and away at university."

Jenn blinked, her own confusion mirroring theirs. "Oh… is he maybe a nephew or a relative or something? We just assumed he'd come through the gap in the fence," she said, her voice faltering slightly.

Brian and Linda shook their heads.

"There haven't been any young kids in this street since ours were small," Linda said, her tone thoughtful.

"Oh… I see," Jenn replied, feeling a nervous flutter in her chest. "Well, not to worry. I'm sure he'll pop by again to play with the girls, and when he does, I'll ask him where he lives." She forced a smile. "I'd better go now and see what carnage is unfolding in the house. It was lovely to finally meet you both!"

"It was nice to meet you too, Jenn," Linda told her. "If you ever need anything, just pop by and ask."

"Thanks, I will. Bye then," she replied with a smile.

Once in the house, Jenn leaned against the closed door, taking a moment to think. A strange, unexplainable feeling had just washed over her.

Shaking it off, she snapped herself back to reality and took off her shoes and jacket. As she glanced around the hallway, her eyes landed on the picture frames. Every single one was askew once again.

Jenn closed her eyes and let out a long sigh before going to straighten them, one by one.

***

At 1:44 am, early Thursday morning, David was awoken by a strange noise coming from somewhere in the house. He glanced over at Jenn, who was still in a deep sleep.

Throwing the duvet off, he got out of bed and headed for the bedroom door. Stepping onto the landing, he cocked his head to one side, trying to pinpoint the source of the mysterious sound.

Click... click... click...

The noise was familiar, but David couldn't quite place it.

Click... click... click...

Opening the baby gate, he descended a couple of stairs and paused, listening intently.

Click... click... click...

Suddenly, it hit him – the sound was unmistakable. It was the distinct noise of a light switch being clicked on and off. However, no light seemed to be coming from anywhere in the house.

A cold unease crept over him as he continued down the stairs. The clicking had now stopped, leaving the house eerily silent. He checked every room but found nothing amiss. No lights had been turned on.

Standing in the kitchen, David's eyes flickered around the room, his ears straining for the faintest sound. The stillness pressed in on him, and he couldn't shake the unnerving feeling that he was being watched, sending a freezing cold shiver down his spine.

He tried to shake off the feeling as he hurried back up the stairs and got back into bed with Jenn, who was still sound asleep.

As for David, he didn't get much sleep that night. He decided it was best to keep this to himself. There was no point in telling Jenn – she'd undoubtedly latch onto the idea that it was some ghostly presence. And the truth was, he didn't want to admit how much it had unnerved him.

***

It was a miserable, wet Wednesday morning, and David and Jenn were trying to get the kids ready for school.

Bella was being a diva about something or other, while Olivia was having a tantrum over the trainers she refused to wear to nursery.

David finally managed to wrestle the kids into their jackets in the hallway, only for them to bolt back into the living room. He rolled his eyes and sighed. Then, as he opened the front door, he took a step back in surprise.

The wheelie bin he'd left out on the kerb the night before was now right outside the front door.

He stood there for a moment, trying to process what he was seeing. How had it got there?!

"Right – come on, kids, let's go! We're running late!" Jenn shouted as she hurried down the stairs. She stopped in her tracks when she saw David standing in the doorway, staring at the bin. "What's that doing there? I thought you took it out last night?" she asked, frowning.

David turned to face her, his expression puzzled. "I did take it out last night… I left it at the kerb…"

"Maybe the bin men have already emptied it," Jenn suggested.

David stepped out into the rain and opened the lid to check. It was still full.

Jenn joined him in the doorway. "That's weird… maybe the wind blew it back here during the night?"

David shook his head slowly. "Nah, it's too heavy for that. Besides, there wasn't any wind last night…" He thought for a moment. "It's probably just some teenagers playing a prank or something. We should invest in a CCTV system."

Jenn nodded, still looking uneasy. "Good idea. I'll check Amazon later and see what I can find." She took a deep breath and turned back to the house. "Right, kids – come on, let's go!" She barely got the last word out before descending into a coughing fit.

The kids came running in from the living room, and Jenn got them into the car while David returned the wheelie bin to the kerb.

Later that evening, Jenn ordered a CCTV system online, which arrived the next day.

David set to work installing it that evening; the setup was pretty straightforward and only took him an hour or so. He drilled a hole through the PVC doorframe, fed the camera's power cable through, and plugged it into the mains socket next to the front door in the hallway. Then, carefully, he tacked the cable neatly around the frame for a clean finish. Next, he positioned the camera just below the stone lintel and secured it with a couple of raw plugs and screws above the front door. The camera now provided a full view of the driveway, the side of the garage, and part of the house.

Using the smartphone app, David synced the system and configured the motion detection zones, adjusting their sensitivity to avoid unnecessary alerts. Everything was working perfectly. He could now see anyone who walked up the driveway.

Meanwhile, the kids were playing upstairs, being as hyper as ever. Olivia, being the youngest, was the most energetic and had little sense of danger. David and Jenn often joked that if Olivia had been born first, they might not have had any more kids.

That afternoon, Jenn walked into the kids' bedroom and froze. Olivia was hanging off the top bunk bed, her legs swinging, pretending to be a monkey. Bella was laughing hysterically.

It was safe to say Olivia never tried that again.

Once David finished installing the CCTV system, Jenn insisted he separate the bunk beds into two single beds, positioned in opposite corners of the room. After Jenn had rearranged and organised the rest of the space, it actually made the room feel bigger.

***

Jenn and David were in the usual morning rush, getting

the kids ready for school and nursery. Jenn sat on the couch, facing the back door, with Olivia on her lap as she carefully plaited her hair. David was helping Bella with her school tie.

Suddenly, Olivia's eyes widened, and she pointed towards the garden. "Look! Who's that, Mummy?" she asked, her small voice curious.

Jenn glanced up, frowning in confusion. "Olivia, what are you pointing at, sweetheart?"

"The man in the garden, Mummy…"

"I saw him too!" Bella shrieked, her voice high with alarm.

David and Jenn shot each other a look.

Without a word, David stood and walked over to the window, peering out. "I don't see anyone…"

"He just walked around the house, and he was smoking," Bella said earnestly.

"Yeah!" Olivia chimed in. "He walked around the corner!"

David's jaw tightened. He strode to the back door, opened it, and stepped outside, the chilly morning air hitting him as he crept cautiously into the garden, looking around. But there was no one there. He walked around the corner of the house. The gate was still closed and locked. Everything was as it should be.

David then returned inside, closing and locking the door behind him. "There was no one out there, darling," he said. "Are you sure it wasn't just your imagination?"

Olivia shook her head firmly. "No, I definitely saw him. He was dressed in black!"

David and Jenn exchanged another look of concern. Still, David decided to play it down.

"Maybe it was just the window cleaner checking if our windows needed cleaning again," he suggested lightly. "Now, come on, we're going to be late. Let's all get our shoes on and head out to the car."

The kids did as they were told, heading into the hallway.

For a moment, David lingered by the window, looking out onto the garden.

Jenn walked up beside him, her expression uneasy. "Don't you think that was weird, David? I've heard that kids can see things we can't…"

David sighed, his shoulders dropping. "Yes, I agree with you – it was weird. But I really don't think it was a ghost she saw. I think it was just their imaginations running wild like usual."

Jenn sighed, unconvinced. "One of these days, I'll make a believer out of you."

David turned to her with a grin. "And maybe, one of these days, I'll make a Belieber out of you!" Then, before Jenn could respond, he launched into a silly dance, singing Justin Bieber's 'What Do You Mean?' at the top of his voice.

"What do you mean? Said you're runnin' outta time… what do you mean…?"

Jenn pressed her lips together, trying not to laugh, though her voice betrayed her amusement. "Oh my God, David, please stop. It's far too early in the morning for this."

David chuckled. "Aw, come on, Jenn – you *love* Justin Bieber!"

"I *hate* Justin Bieber! I can't stand him!" she shot back, rolling her eyes.

David grinned mischievously. "Well, the day you turn me into a believer of ghosts will be the day I turn you into a Justin Bieber-loving Belieber!"

Jenn scoffed. "Well, that's never going to happen!"

David laughed, shaking his head as they headed towards the hallway.

Later that day, Jenn attended her radiology appointment and had the X-ray taken. The radiologist explained that it would take a few weeks for her GP to receive the results and get in touch.

Chapter 5

Slowly but surely, their house was starting to feel more like a home. David had now painted most of the rooms, starting with the kids' bedroom. He had dismantled the hideous brown fitted wardrobes in his and Jenn's bedroom and now the room felt a lot bigger, all that he had to do now was paint the room. Jenn had decided on brilliant white throughout the house for a fresh, clean look.

David had also laid laminate flooring in both the kids' room, the box room and the upstairs landing. Jenn had plans to turn the box room into a playroom where the kids could store all their toys.

They had also managed to get a great deal on a new kitchen from a local merchant. The merchant would supply and fit the kitchen, but first, David needed to rip out the old one himself.

David didn't mind – doing it himself saved a couple of hundred quid and gave him a good workout.

As he pulled out the old units, David uncovered

years of junk and rubbish hidden under the kickboards. Among the debris, he found old scraps of paper, bottle caps, and tiny Micro Machines toy cars. Then, something caught his eye: an old receipt book, covered in dust and grime. Curious, he blew the dust off and wiped the cover with his hand, revealing the name of the company: *'Thompson and Sons Auction House.'*

David flipped through the book, briefly studying the faded receipt stubs. After a moment, he shrugged and tossed it in the bin – along with all the other junk he'd found – and carried on with his task. There was still plenty to do, especially as the kitchen fitter was coming first thing in the morning to install the new kitchen.

This time tomorrow, the kitchen wouldn't look quite so much like a building site, he hoped.

***

It was a beautiful, sunny Saturday afternoon, and Jenn was in the kitchen making dinner, the windows open to let in the fresh air. The kids were playing in the garden with their friend Andy, crouched in a circle at the bottom of the lawn, seemingly digging for worms.

David – who'd been pottering about in the garage – emerged with three big trough-style planters stacked under one arm and a huge bag of compost in the other. Gardening was one of David's favourite hobbies. He loved teaching the kids about nature and often got them involved, hoping to instil an appreciation for healthy eating and the satisfaction of growing their own vegetables.

"Hey, kids!" he called, his voice carrying across the garden.

All three children looked up from their makeshift digging project.

"Do you want to help me plant some seeds?" he asked, his tone inviting.

"Yeah!" they all replied excitedly, jumping up and running over to the patio.

David placed the planters down, opened the bag of compost, and began filling each trough before levelling the soil off neatly. He then stood up and reached into the back pocket of his jeans, pulling out three packets of seeds.

"OK, kids," he began, holding up the packets so they could see. "We're going to plant sunflowers in this one." He pointed to the first planter. "Lavender in this one," he continued, motioning to the second, "and sweet peas in the last one."

The kids crowded around him eagerly.

David poured the sunflower seeds into his hand and held them out for the kids. "OK, take a few seeds each," he instructed.

The children eagerly reached out, grabbing seeds with excited hands.

"Now, what we need to do is drop them onto the soil."

The kids did as they were told and carefully scattered their seeds across the surface of the soil.

"Great," David said. "Now, gently press them into the soil – not too deep – and cover them lightly with the excess soil."

The children followed his instructions, giggling as they patted the seeds into place. They repeated this process with the other two planters until all the seeds were planted.

"Great job, kids!" David beamed. "Now, after a couple of weeks, when the plants have grown a bit, bumblebees will come to pollinate them and then move on to other plants in the area."

"To make honey!" Olivia shouted, her eyes lighting up.

David laughed. "That's right, Olivia. To make honey. That's why we should always look after bumblebees, because-"

"They look after us!" Bella interrupted proudly.

Andy frowned, tilting his head as he looked up at David. "How do the bees look after us?" he asked, his curiosity piqued.

David crouched down to Andy's level and smiled warmly. "Because," he explained, "when bees fly around collecting pollen from flowers, lots of different pollen gets stuck to their legs and bodies. Then, when they land on other flowers and plants, they spread that pollen around, which helps them grow."

Andy still looked confused. "But how does that help *us*?" he asked.

David smiled patiently and continued, "Because they help pollinate crops like wheat and corn, and when farmers harvest those crops, that's how we get our food. Wheat gets turned into flour to make bread, and corn becomes corn flakes and lots of other things. So, if we didn't have any bees, we wouldn't have as much food to eat. That's why it's so important to look after the bees."

Andy's face lit up in amazement. "Oh, I see!" he exclaimed. "That's amazing – they're like superheroes!"

David chuckled. "Exactly! If I could be anything in the world, I would be a bumblebee!"

"Me too!" Andy cried with enthusiasm.

Just then, Jenn stepped out onto the patio, carrying a tray of chocolate biscuits and juice for the kids. "Right! Who wants juice and biscuits?"

"Yay! We do! We do!" Bella and Olivia cried, jumping up and down in excitement.

Jenn glanced around and frowned. "Where's Andy gone?" she asked. "I wanted to ask him about his parents."

David looked up from the tray of biscuits. "That's strange… he was literally here a second ago."

"Yeah, he does that sometimes," Bella said nonchalantly, picking up a biscuit and shoving it into her mouth. Olivia nodded in agreement, her mouth already full.

David and Jenn exchanged a confused glance.

"Oh well, maybe he had to go home… more biscuits for me then!" Chuckling, David picked up a biscuit and popped it in his mouth, grinning at the girls.

Bella and Olivia giggled at their dad's antics.

"Come on, girls," David said after a moment. "Let's go and water our seeds."

As the kids nodded eagerly, Jenn pulled David aside. "Look, David, I forgot to tell you this before, but I spoke to the neighbours and Andy isn't theirs. He doesn't live next door. In fact, they've never even heard of him. Their children are grown up and away at university."

David scratched his chin. "That's strange…" he murmured.

"Yeah," Jenn continued, "they said there haven't been any kids living on this street since their kids were young."

David raised his eyebrows, his expression thoughtful. "Hmm… that's very strange. Well, next time we see him, we'll just ask where he lives. I'm sure his parents must wonder where he disappears to when he's playing with the girls in our garden."

Jenn nodded in agreement. "You would think…"

***

Sunday morning, the kids woke up early as usual. However, instead of rushing to their parents, they decided to play quietly in the small box room that Jenn had recently turned into a toy room.

David and Jenn, meanwhile, were savouring a rare lie-in together, basking in the peace and quiet while sleepily listening for the inevitable squabble to break out.

Unbeknownst to them, Bella had cleverly figured out how to escape their bedroom without disturbing their parents. She would flip her metal Disney Princess wastepaper bin upside down and place it in front of the baby gate across their bedroom door. Using it as a step, she could carefully climb over the gate. Then, she'd coax Olivia into doing the same, even lifting her little sister over the gate when needed. Free from their confinement, the two would happily play in the toy room without disturbing David or Jenn.

That morning, as the kids played on the floor with

their Barbie dolls, Olivia suddenly needed to use the toilet. So, scrambling to her feet, she rushed to the bathroom, which was directly across from their bedroom. "Hey!" she cried, stopping in her tracks. "Who opened the gate and turned on the light?"

Jenn's eyes snapped open. She glanced at David, who was lying on his side, facing her. He too opened his eyes and met hers with a confused look. A terrible feeling washed over Jenn as she threw the duvet off, got out of bed, and hurried to investigate.

Sure enough, the kids' bedroom light was on, and the baby gate stood wide open.

Jenn stepped cautiously into the kids' bedroom, a strange, eerie sensation creeping over her. By this time, David had followed her out of bed and into the room. Olivia had gone into the bathroom. Bella had appeared in the hallway, holding one of her dolls, her expression curious.

The baby gate in question was simple in design: a sturdy, spring-loaded bi-folding gate made of durable plastic. Unlocking the gate required a precise set of movements that were far too complicated for small children. You had to pull a small slide at the top back with your thumb, push it down, and release the locking mechanism in one smooth motion. If done incorrectly, the gate wouldn't budge.

David had installed it about two inches from the floor, making it the perfect height to stop the kids from escaping – or so he thought.

Jenn went over to Bella and knelt down to her level.

"Bella, sweetheart, did you open the baby gate this morning?"

Bella looked her mum straight in the eye. "No, Mummy," she said, shaking her head. "I can't open the gate. That's why I used my bin as a step and climbed over." She pointed to her bin, which was still exactly where she'd left it.

Jenn turned to look at the bin, then back at Bella. "I know, sweetie," she said softly. "It's OK if you did open the gate. Mummy and Daddy aren't angry with you; we just want you to tell us the truth, OK?"

Bella rolled her eyes and huffed. "I just *did* tell you, Mummy. I can't open the gate – that's why I used my bin as a step."

The sound of the toilet flushing broke the tension, and Olivia came out of the bathroom, singing a little song to herself.

"Oliva, did you wash your hands?" David asked, raising an eyebrow.

Olivia stopped in her tracks and turned to look at him.

David stared back and, after a moment, Olivia rolled her eyes, sighed loudly, and walked back into the bathroom to wash her hands.

Bella, uninterested in the whole gate thing, walked back into the toy room and resumed playing with her dolls.

Slowly, Jenn stood up and turned to David, her expression a mix of confusion and concern. She had one of her 'how-do-you-explain-this?' looks on her face.

David rubbed the sleep out of his eyes and sighed

deeply. "Please don't say it, Jenn. I can't be bothered to have the same discussion with you over and over again."

Jenn's voice was quiet but firm as she whispered, "Well, how do you explain this then, David?" She motioned towards the open gate and light switch, her gaze hardening. "The gate can't just open on its own, can it?"

David looked at the scene, trying to make sense of it. "Well," he began slowly, "as Bella was climbing over the gate, she must have somehow opened it in the process."

Jenn glared at David. "And how the hell can she do that, Columbo? She's only small! Plus, don't you think Olivia would have told us by now if her big sister managed to do all that? You know what they're like with telling tales on each other!"

David rubbed his face again, eyes squinting against the morning light, before stretching his arms wide. Then, he hunched over, feeling his back crack with a satisfying sigh. "Jenn," he said, still slightly exasperated, "if you think it was a ghost or goblin – or whatever the hell you think opened the gate and turned the light on – that's fine. I'm not going to tell you otherwise. But I just don't understand what you want me to do about it."

"I just want you to wake up and see that there's something going on in this house – and it's giving me the creeps!" Jenn replied, her voice quieter but firm.

David sighed, his frustration melting into weariness as he slowly walked over to Jenn. He put his arms around her waist and gave her a reassuring hug. "Look, Jenn," he said softly, "all I'm saying is, nine times out of ten, there's a reasonable explanation for everything. We just have to find it. Now, would you like a coffee? I'm going downstairs with the kids to make them some breakfast."

"That would be nice, thank you," Jenn replied, her tone still tinged with unease. "But I'm getting one of those video baby monitors, and I don't care what you say!"

David switched into humour mode, his grin returning. "OK, darling, whatever you think is best." He then turned and shouted, "Come, on kids! Daddy's going downstairs to make breakfast!"

The kids squealed with excitement and raced downstairs, their footsteps echoing through the house as David followed.

Once they were gone, Jenn looked slowly around the room, the same unsettling feeling creeping over her. A cold shiver ran down her spine, as if someone was watching her. Quickly, she hurried out of the room, turning the light off as she went and closing the door behind her.

Later that afternoon, Jenn went on Amazon to look for video baby monitors, and after browsing for a while, she eventually found one that caught her eye. It was top of the line, with HD night vision and crystal-clear digital sound speakers. She ordered it, and a few days later, it arrived.

When the package came, she wasted no time. She set it up in the kids' room, plugging the camera into the mains and positioning it for a full view of the room. Once everything was in place, she synced the monitor to her phone and placed it next to her bedside table, ready for the night.

***

It was Monday morning. David was downstairs with the kids, giving them their breakfasts and trying to get them ready for school and nursery. Jenn was upstairs in the bedroom. She had just come out of the shower and was now getting dressed at her side of the bed. The curtains were drawn at the window.

Suddenly, she heard a faint scratching noise behind her, and when she turned around, she gasped.

The print that David and the kids had given her for Mother's Day – the one hanging above the TV – was slowly swinging, all on its own. The hairs on the back of Jenn's neck stood up as a chill of fear washed over her. She took a small step back, her eyes fixed on the swinging frame. She couldn't believe what she was seeing.

Then, the frame stopped abruptly, causing Jenn to gasp once more as she stepped back even further. Her stomach was in knots. She didn't know what to make of it. Still fixated on the frame, she slowly approached it, inspecting it closely.

Gently, she nudged the bottom right corner with her finger, and the frame began to swing again, slowly coming to a natural stop.

Jenn carefully took the frame off the wall and inspected the back, checking the nail it hung from. Everything seemed normal – nothing out of the ordinary. There was no draught coming from anywhere, and she was the only one in the room, standing nowhere near the print. So, how had it been moving on its own?

She hoped it was some sort of prank, maybe one of

David's elaborate jokes. So, she checked again, but there was nothing.

Frustrated but still unsettled, she hung the frame back on the nail and quickly finished getting dressed.

She was really freaked out.

Once she was done, Jenn hurried over to the window, opened the curtains, and then rushed to the door. As she switched off the bedroom light and closed the door behind her, a cold shiver ran down her spine.

A few moments later, she heard it.

The frame had begun to swing again.

***

It was 2:34 am on a Tuesday morning when David sleepily got up to use the bathroom. He didn't bother turning on the light; the faint glow from the streetlights outside provided just enough illumination to see what he was doing. He also didn't bother flushing the toilet, not wanting to wake up the rest of the house. So, instead, he just closed the toilet lid, washed his hands quickly, and headed back to the bedroom.

Click... click... click...

David froze. The hairs on the back of his neck stood up, and his heart began to race. His eyes widened as he held his breath for a moment, straining to hear the sound again.

Click... click... click...

This time, the clicking was louder and seemed closer.

Slowly, David turned around, his eyes fixed on the bathroom light.

Then, he saw it.

Click… click…

The switch clicked slowly, as if some invisible force were toying with it. However, the bathroom light didn't turn on – and nor did the extractor fan that was wired up to the light.

David's mind raced, his heart pounding in his chest as fear gripped him completely. His body was in full fight-or-flight mode, his mouth going dry as adrenaline surged through his veins.

What was he seeing? Was this some kind of paranormal experience? Or was it just his imagination?

He didn't know, but in that moment, something inside him snapped him out of the trance. He took a deep breath and stepped towards the light switch, his fingers trembling as he turned the bathroom light on. Bright light flooded the landing, and David squinted as his night vision was obliterated by the sudden glare.

He scanned the hallway quickly, then stepped into the bathroom.

Just as he'd suspected, nothing was out of place.

David sighed and shook his head. He'd chalk this up to being dog-tired and imagining things in his sleepy state.

With that, he returned to the bedroom and got back into bed. But he couldn't sleep; he just kept picturing that light switch, turning on and off and on and off…

Chapter 6

David had finished his visits for the day and was heading home to type up his notes. He reversed the car into the driveway, put it in park, and got out. As he pressed the immobiliser to lock the car, he stretched his arms and arched his back. His lower back cracked, and he let out a satisfying sigh. After putting the car keys into the right pocket of his combat trousers, he reached into his left pocket to grab his house keys.

He took two steps towards the front door, then stopped in his tracks.

The gate at the side of the house, which led to the back garden, was wide open. And, standing just beyond it was a large black dog, staring directly at him.

David froze, a cold shiver creeping down his spine. The dog was tall, with a muscular build. It appeared to be male, and from the looks of it, it resembled an American Pit Bull, though David couldn't be sure. Its eyes were a piercing green, unnervingly intense, and its black coat was sleek and shiny, like a panther's.

But what terrified David the most was the blood dripping from its mouth.

The dog growled low in its throat, showing off its sharp, bloodstained teeth. David didn't know if it was rabid or had just killed something, but his gut told him it was the latter.

Instinctively, David raised his hands in front of him, palms out, trying to show the dog that he wasn't a threat and that he meant no harm. "Hello, pup," he said softly, "where did you come from?"

The dog took a slow step forwards, its growl deepening, its snarl growing louder.

"Good boy… it's OK… I'm not going to hurt you…" David murmured, hoping to calm it down.

Suddenly, the dog started barking, making David jump. Heart pounding, he quickly reached into his pocket to retrieve his car keys, pressing the immobiliser button to unlock the car. He then opened the driver's side door just a crack. The dog was now only about four feet away. David knew he had to get away from this thing – fast.

It's now or never, he thought as he opened the door just wide enough to quickly slip inside. He slammed the door shut just as the dog lunged at him.

The dog jumped up at the window, standing on its hind legs, barking and snarling aggressively. One of its front paws was pressed against the window, its claws scraping against the glass.

David noticed that one of its front toes was missing on the left paw. *Probably lost it in a fight with another dog,* he thought, his heart still racing.

The dog continued barking, its snarls growing louder.

David reached into his pocket to grab his phone, and just as he was about to unlock the screen, the dog became even more agitated. It reared back on its hind legs and threw its weight against the car. The vehicle lurched violently from side to side, so much so that David's phone slipped from his hand and fell into the passenger footwell.

"Jesus! Why don't you just piss off, you great ugly bastard!" he shouted, his frustration boiling over as he quickly leaned down to retrieve his phone.

By the time he sat back up, the barking had stopped.

David looked around, but the dog was nowhere to be seen.

His confusion grew. *Where did it go? It couldn't have just disappeared!* Maybe it saw a squirrel or something and decided to chase that instead of terrorising him, he reasoned, though the thought didn't sit well with him at all.

Suddenly, David remembered the brand-new walking stick he'd been using with a patient earlier that day – it was lying on the back seat. He grabbed it, slipping it out of the cellophane wrapping before adjusting it to the highest setting to make it longer. At least – if the devil dog was still lurking out there, ready to pounce – David would be able to put a bit of distance between them. Plus, he could use the stick to defend himself.

Slowly, David opened the door and looked around. The dog was still nowhere to be seen. He slowly crept around the car, holding the walking stick over his right shoulder like a baseball player ready to take a swing. He checked every corner, scanning for any sign of movement, and a sigh of relief escaped him as he saw no sign of the dog. Then, he walked cautiously out of the driveway and looked both ways down the street.

The silence was unnerving. The street was eerily quiet, not a soul in sight.

David started to wonder, his mind racing with thoughts such as, *Where did the blood around its mouth come from? And why was our gate open?*

Curiosity gnawed at him as he made his way around to the back garden, past the small plastic storage box where he kept his gardening tools and the kids' scooters. He continued past the neatly lined-up wheelie bins, then around the corner to the garden.

Slowly, he peered around the corner of the extension, scanning the entire area. Nothing seemed out of place. The kids' toys were still scattered about in the same spots they'd left them.

He relaxed slightly and lowered the walking stick by his side, continuing to scan the garden.

Then, just as he was about to head inside, something caught his eye at the bottom of the garden, near the kids' Wendy house.

At first, he couldn't make out what it was, but as he got closer, his heart sank.

It was Lola.

She was lying motionless, her body covered in blood. Her throat had been slashed, and there were deep wounds in her stomach.

David's hands shook as he dropped the walking stick, collapsing to his knees in shock.

"No!" he screamed, his voice raw with grief as he gently picked up her lifeless body and cradled it to his chest. She was still warm. Sobbing uncontrollably, he hugged and kissed his beloved pet's head as he slowly rocked back and forth.

As tears fell down from David's cheeks and splashed on his dead cat, he tried to calm himself by taking several deep breaths. "I'll be back in a minute, sweetheart…OK? I'm going to get you a blanket."

With trembling hands, he slowly placed Lola down on the grass and stood up, his work polo shirt now covered in blood. Then, still sobbing quietly, he staggered to his feet, in deep shock. He walked back to the car, opened the boot, and grabbed the red tartan picnic blanket he always kept in there for emergencies. Closing the boot again, he walked back to Lola's body.

Carefully – after falling to his knees again, sobbing at the sorry sight – he placed the blanket on the grass and gently picked Lola up, giving her one last hug before kissing her on the head. "Sleep tight, darling. Don't ever forget how much we all loved you…"

David placed Lola gently in the centre of the blanket, wrapping her up slowly. He then picked her up and cradled her carefully, like a baby. His arms felt heavy as he walked back to the car, his heart aching with every step. After opening the boot and placing her inside, he stood there for a few moments, staring at her still form as tears continued streaming down his face.

He would bury her later, next to Thumper, after he'd broken the news to Jenn and the kids.

He didn't know how he was going to tell Jenn. First the rabbit, now the cat – she was going to be just as distraught as he was.

David was beginning to think this house was cursed.

He knew he had to keep this from the kids; there was no way he could tell them what had really happened, how she'd really died. He'd tell them she'd simply gone to sleep in the garden, napping in the sunshine, and had sadly never woken up.

David slowly closed the boot, his hands still trembling. Only then did he realise they were covered in blood.

I have to get my head together, he thought. *I need to clean up the blood in the garden, then myself, before I go get the kids.*

So, he went over to the garden hose reel, turned the tap, and grabbed the end of the hose. It took a moment or two for the water to come through, and then it shot out in a cold, harsh jet. He held one hand under the hose until it was clean, then switched hands and repeated the process. He then walked to the back of the garden where Lola had died.

In the fog of his grief, he hadn't fully taken in the scene. But now, as he looked around, he realised just how horrific it was. It was a bloodbath – the blood had even splattered all over the kids' plastic Wendy house. It was the kind of thing you would expect to see at a real murder scene.

The large patch of blood where he'd found her was thick, dark, and starting to congeal. She really hadn't stood a chance. The viciousness of the attack was almost too painful to comprehend. He just hoped she hadn't suffered for long.

Tears welled up in David's eyes again as he began to

hose away the blood from the area – including the Wendy house. He worked quickly, almost mechanically, as if on autopilot, and while it only took him about five minutes to clean the place up, it felt like hours. He just couldn't believe Lola was gone. He kept thinking how terrified she must have been.

He was about to turn away when he noticed the walking stick he'd dropped earlier, now also covered in blood. He picked it up and sprayed it clean with the hose before walking back to the car. He opened the boot again and placed the stick inside.

As David stood there again, staring at Lola's tiny body, wrapped up in the blanket, he was suddenly overcome with a surge of anger. Whose bastard devil dog was roaming around the neighbourhood, killing defenceless animals? And more importantly, where had it gone?

David had always been an animal lover, and he'd never bought into the idea of 'dangerous breeds' of dogs, like Staffordshire Bull Terriers or XL Bullies. He had always believed that it was the way they were raised, not the breed itself. But this dog was different. David had been able to sense the bloodlust in it. He'd seen the evil in its eyes. It had clearly been bred to be a fierce killing machine. He just kept thinking, *What if it had got a hold of one of the kids?* The idea made his stomach twist. It really didn't bear thinking about.

One thing he knew for sure: if that dog ever came back again, he wouldn't hesitate to kill it.

After one last look at the blanket, David slammed the boot shut, his hands still shaking with rage. He went into the house, stripped off his bloody clothes, and tossed them into the washing machine. Then he went upstairs for a shower, trying to wash away the horror.

He still had a lot of patient notes to type up for the day, but given the circumstances, they were the least of his worries. Right now, he had to go pick up the kids.

As he drove to school, David's mind raced. *How did the dog get into the garden? And who opened the gate?* He knew for sure it had been closed when they left this morning.

After a while, he pulled into the school car park and switched off the engine. Then he pulled out his phone and opened the CCTV app, scrolling through all the notifications the camera had picked up throughout the day.

8:02 am – David, Jenn, and the kids got in the car and left for the day.

10:13 am – The postman put several letters through the door.

1:33 pm – A delivery driver arrived with a parcel. After a few moments, he realised no one was home. He looked around, saw the gate, opened it, and walked through.

David watched the video intently. He could hear the delivery driver open the plastic storage box behind the garage, then close it again. A moment later, the driver strolled out and got back in his van, unaware that he'd left the gate open.

David was just about to press play on the next video when he suddenly heard...

Tap... tap... tap...

He nearly jumped out of his skin, then quickly looked up to see where the noise had come from. It was one of Bella's after-school teachers, knocking on the passenger side window, greeting him with a huge smile.

"Hi, David! How are you? I've not seen you for ages!" she said cheerily.

David smiled back, pressing the button to wind down the passenger side window. "Hi, Kelly. Yeah, it's been a while… How are you?" he asked, trying to sound casual.

"Oh, I'm fine. Same old, same old. Another day, another dollar," she replied, still smiling. "Do you want me to go in and get Bella for you?"

"Yeah, that would be great. Thanks, Kelly," David replied, slipping his phone back into his pocket.

A few minutes later, Kelly brought Bella out, and David helped her into the car.

He knew he had to act like it was any other day, even though his heart was breaking – after all, he was driving around with the family pet cat in the boot. But he also knew it was the safest place for Lola at the moment. At least until Jenn got home and they could bury her.

Once Bella was settled in the back, David picked up Olivia from nursery and they all headed home.

When they got inside, David got the kids settled in front of the TV, putting on Netflix to keep them entertained while he made a start on dinner. *Cocomelon* was singing nursery songs, which he thought would keep them occupied for at least a few moments.

David was standing in the kitchen, staring into space, when he heard Jenn put her key in the door.

"Hiya!" she called cheerily. "Sorry I'm late, that bus took ages." She put her work bag down, took her jacket off in the hall, and walked into the kitchen. One look at David, and she knew something was wrong. He looked terrible. He was pale, his eyes red and puffy, and he seemed utterly drained.

Jenn's face fell. "What's up? Where are the kids?" she asked, her voice laced with concern.

He cleared his throat before speaking. "They're fine. They're watching TV," he told her, nodding in the direction of the living room.

Jenn walked further into the kitchen, her concern growing. She peeked into the living room and said, "Hi, girls… how was school and nursery?"

The kids grunted and mumbled in response, too absorbed in the TV to answer properly.

Jenn turned her attention back to David. "Honey, what's wrong? Are you OK? What's happened?"

David's eyes welled up again, and he seemed unable to hold back the flood of emotion. "It would be better if I just showed you," he said quietly, his voice trembling. "Come with me."

With that, he grabbed his car keys from the kitchen worktop and headed for the front door, motioning for Jenn to follow.

"Girls, Mummy and Daddy will be back in a minute, OK?" Jenn received another grunt and mumble from the kids as she quickly followed David outside.

David unlocked the car with the immobiliser, opened the boot, and stood with his hands in his pockets, staring down at the ground.

"David, what's going on? You're really scaring me now…" Jenn looked into the boot and saw the wrapped-up blanket. "What's that?" she asked, her voice trembling with fear.

David sighed as a tear rolled down his cheek. "It's Lola," he said quietly. "When I came home from work this afternoon, the gate was open, and a huge, aggressive black dog wandered through it, blood dripping from its mouth…"

Jenn's hand flew to her lips as she began to cry. "Oh my God… how did it get in?" she asked, her voice cracking.

"A delivery driver put a parcel in the storage box and left the gate open," David explained. "It must have wandered in after that."

Jenn slowly leaned into the boot, her hand shaking as she gently unwrapped the blanket to reveal Lola's dead body. "Oh my God, my poor cat!" she cried hysterically.

David pulled her close, holding her as she sobbed uncontrollably into his shoulder. "I know, darling… don't worry… everything will be OK," he whispered, kissing her forehead.

Jenn started to cough, and after a moment, she tried to compose herself by taking several deep breaths. David went over to the driver's side door, opened it, and grabbed a handful of tissues from the door pocket, handing them to Jenn to dry her tears.

After a moment, Jenn turned to David, her voice trembling. "Where did this dog go? And where did it come from?" she asked. "What if it attacks a child?!"

David sighed deeply, rubbing his face in frustration. "I don't know where it went, Jenn. Or where it came from. Like I said, I came home from work, got out of the car, and looked up to see it standing by the open gate, growling and snarling at me. I'm pretty sure it was going to attack, so I got back into the car. It jumped up on its back legs and was barking at me through the window. So, I pulled my phone out to film the ugly big bastard and maybe call the police, but it jerked the car and I dropped my phone. By the time I picked it up, the dog was gone, and I didn't see where it went."

Jenn's eyes widened in shock. "Jesus Christ... what did this dog look like?"

"It was huge – all muscle – with green eyes, and a short, black, smooth coat. It also had a toe missing on its front paw."

Jenn frowned. "A toe missing? How do you know that?"

"Because it put its front paws on the window when it was trying to get to me," David told her. "It probably scratched the door panel, too; I haven't had a chance to check yet." With that, he walked over to inspect the driver's side door. Sure enough, there were several deep, heavy scratches on the paintwork, just below the window. "Look... come and have a look at the state of my door," he said, motioning for Jenn to come closer.

Jenn went over to the car door, staring in disbelief at the scratches. "Oh my God..."

David pulled his phone out of his pocket and opened the CCTV app, searching for the clip from when he arrived home that afternoon. "Look," he said, handing Jenn his phone. "See for yourself... it was a monster of a thing!"

Jenn watched the video intently and, after a few

moments, she screwed up her face in confusion. "David, what the hell are you doing here? I don't see any dog…"

David frowned, genuinely puzzled. "What? What are you talking about? It's right there – the camera caught it all!"

"Have you actually watched the video?" she asked.

"Not yet, no. I've had to deal with a lot of shit this afternoon," he replied, exasperated. "I don't need to see it anyway; I was there."

"Well, all I see is you coming home, acting weird, getting out of the car with a walking stick, disappearing out of frame, and then coming back to the car covered in blood…" She trailed off, studying his face.

"What are you talking about, Jenn? The dog is right there!" David exclaimed, his voice rising in frustration.

"See for yourself," she replied, giving him his phone back.

David replayed the video. He watched as he reversed into the driveway, got out of the car, walked a couple of steps, and stopped in his tracks. He raised his hands, palms up, and then slowly walked back to the car, getting in. Jenn was right – there was no dog in sight.

"W-what?" he spluttered. "There was a big black dog there, Jenn…"

"Well, I didn't see a dog, David!"

"Well, what the hell do you think I'm reacting to in the video?" he snapped, his confusion and frustration mounting.

David continued watching the video. He saw himself get out of the car with the walking stick, carefully searching for something. Then he walked out of the frame, only to return a few moments later, clearly distraught and covered in blood.

"What the fuck is going on?!" he muttered. "Jenn, I swear to God, there was a dog in this very driveway, and it killed Lola in the garden!"

Jenn suddenly became very uneasy; David could see it in her face.

"OK…" she said, her voice trembling.

"What? What are you giving me that look for, Jenn?" David asked, his tone sharp.

"Nothing, I'm not giving you any look… I just…" She trailed off.

"You just what?"

"I don't know," she replied, her voice strained. "You've told me something, and I've just watched a video that proves otherwise. What else am I meant to think?"

David scoffed in disbelief. "What? You really think I would kill my own cat? Our family pet? The one I loved like one of our children? Is that honestly what you think, Jenn?"

"No… well… I don't know, David…"

David rubbed his face, frustration boiling over as he started to laugh, though there was zero humour in it. "OK then," he said, shaking his head, "let's say you're right. Let's say I'm some kind of sicko who would actually do something like that. How the fuck would I be able to disembowel a cat and cut its throat with a fucking walking stick?!"

"I don't know, David!" Jenn snapped. "Just like you can't explain why the dog in question is nowhere to be seen on that video…" Jenn's words trailed off as she started to cry, her emotions unravelling. The more worked up she became, the more she coughed, her chest tight with the effort.

David sighed as he closed the boot. "OK… that's fine, believe whatever you want. But I think it would be better if we told the kids she went peacefully while she was sleeping in the garden, rather than telling them that their daddy went all Jack Torrance and butchered her to death with a walking stick!" With that, he locked the car and went back into the house.

Jenn closed her eyes, sighed, and shook her head.

After dinner, David and Jenn sat the kids down and told them that their beloved cat had gone for a lie-down in the garden and never woke up. They also told them that she was now playing with her best friend, Thumper, in Heaven.

The kids didn't take it well. They couldn't understand why their pets kept going to Heaven and leaving them.

Eventually, the girls picked out a spot next to Thumper, and they buried Lola there. They placed her favourite toys in the grave and said goodbye. It was a tough day for everyone.

Later that night, David and Jenn lay in bed, unable to sleep. They were both lying on their sides with their backs to each other, an uncomfortable silence between them. Jenn didn't know what to make of what she'd seen in the video earlier, and David didn't know how to process the events of that afternoon.

Jenn picked up her phone to check the time. It was 11:59 pm. As she swiped left to the next page of her home screen, a 24-hour digital clock appeared, and she watched the seconds tick by.

"Five... four... three... two... one... and..." She pointed to the bedroom door as it suddenly began to rattle violently.

David quickly sat up in bed, startled. "What the hell was that?" he asked.

"That's the bedroom door handle rattling. It happens every night at the exact same time," she replied.

Confused, David looked at his smartwatch and then at Jenn. "What? What are you talking about, every night? I've never heard anything before..."

"That's because you're usually sleeping by this time, David. That door has rattled like that every night at the same time since we moved in here."

David cleared his throat. "Well, maybe it's just a draught or something," he said.

Jenn scoffed. "A draught? Yeah, that's probably what it is. Every night, at exactly the same time, a draught blows through the house, because there's always a 'perfectly rational explanation' for these things, isn't there, David?"

David was geared up and ready to answer Jenn with a witty remark, though he quickly realised she was baiting him for an argument. So, instead, he decided to take the moral high ground and not rise to her goading. After all, he was too tired and couldn't be bothered verbally sparring with Jenn at this hour.

"Yeah, that's right, sweetheart," he said, turning onto his left side, his back towards Jenn. "Goodnight!"

Jenn scoffed once more. "Whatever, goodnight," she hissed.

The next day, things weren't much better between them. In fact, for a few days after Lola's passing, a dark cloud hung over the entire house.

Chapter 7

Jenn – who was lying on her side, with her back to David – was awoken by the sound of the baby monitor crackling into life; some movement in the kids' room must have activated it. She shifted position, so she was lying on her right elbow, and picked up the monitor, squinting at the bright LCD display as her night vision adjusted.

She couldn't see anything out of the ordinary, just the kids moving about while they slept. She checked the time on her phone – it was 2:38 am.

Jenn was just about to put the monitor back on her bedside table when she noticed something odd – what looked like dust particles floating around the kids, somehow visible on the tiny screen. The particles were moving in a peculiar way, like a huge flock of starlings swooping and diving in all directions. Continuing to study the display, Jenn noticed that whenever the particles came closer to the kids, the girls would react and begin to mumble in their sleep.

Why would dust particles act in this way? And why were they so visible?

Unless, of course, they weren't dust particles at all.

Jenn – who used to watch a lot of paranormal shows – had heard of things called 'light orbs' before. These orbs couldn't be seen with the naked eye, but they could be captured on various recording equipment like cameras and night vision goggles. Light orbs, she knew, usually appeared when a spiritual or paranormal presence was near.

After a few moments of hesitation, Jenn decided to get up and conduct her own little experiment while she checked on the kids. So, being as quiet as she could, she crept out onto the landing, turned the light on, and opened the kids' door, bathing the two girls in light. They were both sleeping soundly.

Slowly, Jenn opened the baby gate across the door, crept into the bedroom, and kissed her daughters on their foreheads. She then left the room just as slowly, closing the door behind her and turning off the landing light.

After returning to her room, she picked up the baby monitor and stared at the screen. Just as she suspected, the 'dust particles' had completely disappeared.

If they had indeed been dust particles, there would be more of them floating around the place when Jenn had entered the room to check on the kids. This proved that they were light orbs and that there was some kind of presence in the house – at least, that's what Jenn thought. What David would think was an entirely different matter.

So, for now, she decided to keep this to herself. She

didn't want David accusing her of overreacting, before inevitably launching into his 'reasonable explanation for everything' speech.

She'd had more than enough of that.

***

It was Saturday afternoon. David was pottering about in the garage, while Jenn was busy tidying the kitchen and following her usual cleaning routine. When she needed to get things done around the house, she would have the kids sit at the table to draw or colour in their colouring books – just as they were doing now.

Jenn had just about finished her tasks when she looked up at the kids, both deep in concentration, and smiled. "Are you OK, girls? What are you drawing?" she asked as she walked over to the kitchen table.

Her blood ran cold when she saw Bella's detailed drawing.

It depicted a dark figure standing in what appeared to be the kids' bedroom, watching them sleep.

"Who's that, Bella?" Jenn asked, her voice faltering a little.

"I don't know, Mummy. He visits us sometimes," Bella replied nonchalantly.

Jenn's heart started racing, and her mouth suddenly became very dry. She cleared her throat. "He visits you in your dreams, you mean?" she asked, trying to steady herself. "Because it looks like you and your sister are sleeping here."

Bella simply shrugged.

Jenn's gaze shifted to Olivia, who was still drawing,

completely unaware of the conversation. It was as though she was in a trance. She was scribbling on the paper, pausing every few moments to pick up a different coloured pencil before scribbling some more. The picture was a dark, swirling mess of black and red, but Olivia had used multiple colours, making the drawing even more unsettling.

"Olivia, what are you drawing, darling?" Jenn asked softly.

Olivia didn't answer; she just kept picking up different pencils and drawing in a clockwise motion.

"Olivia, sweetheart?" Jenn repeated, her voice trembling now.

But, once again, Olivia didn't react. She only picked up speed, her movements becoming ever more frantic.

Panic rose in Jenn's chest. She touched Olivia's shoulders, but her daughter remained locked in her trance, scribbling faster and faster.

"Olivia!" Jenn shouted. "Answer me!"

Startled, Olivia jumped and dropped her pencil. She then turned to Jenn with a confused expression on her face. "What, Mummy?" she asked innocently.

"I was talking to you, and you weren't listening. You just kept drawing," Jenn said, her voice strained with worry.

Olivia rubbed her eyes. "I didn't hear you, Mummy."

Bella began to giggle, and Olivia looked at her, confused, before giggling too – even though she had no idea what she was laughing at.

"What is that you're drawing, darling?" Jenn asked, desperately trying to understand.

"I don't know… I saw it in my dream, Mummy," Olivia replied. With that, she jumped off her chair and toddled off to the kitchen. "What are we having for dinner, Mummy? I'm hungry. Can I get a snack?"

"I want a snack too!" Bella cried, jumping off her chair and following Olivia.

Jenn picked up the two drawings and studied them closely. She couldn't make sense of what she was looking at, but it seemed like some kind of portal. A sinking feeling washed over her, making her skin crawl.

"Mummy… Mummy… Mummy!" Bella shouted, snapping Jenn out of her dark thoughts.

She looked up, startled. "What, Bella?"

"Can we have a biscuit each?" Bella asked eagerly.

Jenn let out a little sigh of relief. "Oh, yes, that's fine… but only one each. I'll be making dinner soon."

The kids began raiding the kitchen cupboards for biscuits, while Jenn went back to staring at the disturbing drawings. After a moment, she went into the kitchen and placed them in the cupboard above the kettle, trying to push aside the unsettling feeling that continued to linger.

***

It was Tuesday afternoon, and David had just finished the last of his visits. He planned to spend the rest of the afternoon typing up his notes before picking up the kids.

On his way home, he realised he'd barely used the bathroom that day, he'd been so busy with patients and meetings. But now, the urgent need to go hit him all at once.

With this in mind, he quickly reversed into the

driveway, jumped out of the car, and rushed up to the front door, unlocking it in a hurry. He then dashed upstairs, practically running to the bathroom. He burst through the door, letting it swing shut behind him, and was about to lift the toilet seat when–

Thud!

It sounded like someone had just pounded on the bathroom door.

"What the fuck was that?" a startled David muttered, a chill running down his spine.

Slowly, he opened the bathroom door and stepped into the hallway. There was no one there, but as his gaze fell on the bathroom door, he gasped.

In the centre of the white-painted door, there was what appeared to be a dirty imprint of a clenched fist. David stared at it for a moment, confused and unsure of what he was seeing.

Stepping closer to the door, he reached out and touched the imprint. His fingers smudged it, and when he inspected his fingertips, it looked like coal dust. An eerie feeling washed over him.

He stepped back into the bathroom. After washing his hands, he grabbed a damp face cloth from beside the sink and walked back to the door, determined to wipe away the imprint.

It came off easily.

David stepped back and studied the door again, his eyes scanning up and down. He then headed out onto the landing and tossed the face cloth into the laundry basket outside his bedroom.

Still, the unsettling feeling lingered.

Something wasn't right here.

What had just happened… had it really happened, or was it just his imagination?

After a moment or so, David shook his head and did what he'd been doing a lot recently whenever he experienced something odd: He dismissed it, thinking there must be some kind of reasonable explanation. Even though he couldn't quite explain it himself, the bottom line was this: He didn't believe in the paranormal, so it couldn't possibly exist.

It was as simple as that.

***

Both David and Jenn were sleeping soundly. David lay on his back, while Jenn lay on her left side, facing him. Suddenly, David snorted and grunted loudly, waking Jenn. She opened her eyes and glared at him with a 'how dare you wake me up with your snoring!' look. It was a look she gave him often – not that he knew about it.

Turning onto her right side, she noticed that the baby monitor had been activated. Glancing at the time, she saw it was 1:32 am.

Jenn picked up the monitor and studied it for a moment. Bella was awake, sitting up with her legs swinging over the bed, while Olivia slept soundly in the other bed.

Frowning, Jenn brought the monitor closer to her face. It appeared that Bella was talking to someone, her head following something around the room. Had she been sleepwalking again? Was she sleep-talking? Jenn had no idea.

Turning up the volume on the monitor, she listened

intently as Bella whispered: "Yes… I go to school… I'm six now… my little sister is still in nursery… erm… I don't know… I like going to the park… drawing and colouring… sometimes Mummy does arts and crafts with us… Mummy and Daddy are sleeping next door…"

Bella pointed towards the camera, making Jenn's stomach churn. Who was she talking to? Or was she just dreaming?

Jenn put the monitor down, threw the duvet off her, and crept out onto the landing. She could still hear Bella whispering.

Turning on the landing light, she opened the kids' bedroom door, causing Bella to gasp and stop mid-sentence. Jenn unlocked the bifold baby gate, and Bella squinted as light flooded the room.

"Bella!" Jenn exclaimed as she stepped over the threshold. "What are you doing out of bed? And who are you talking to?" she asked.

Bella's eyes darted to the corner of the room before quickly returning to her mum.

Jenn frowned and stepped further into the room, glancing in the direction Bella had just looked. There was nothing there.

"Nothing, Mummy… I'm not talking to anyone," Bella told her.

"I just heard you on the monitor, sweetheart. You were whispering about how you like drawing and colouring, and that Mummy and Daddy were sleeping next door. I heard it all."

Bella pulled a face, as if she had just sucked on a

wedge of lemon. "Erm… I don't know… I'm sorry, Mummy," she said sheepishly.

"Were you talking to your imaginary friend?" Jenn asked.

Bella's eyes darted back to the corner of the room and then to her mum again. She nodded slowly.

Once more, Jenn looked over at the corner of the room, a chill creeping up her spine as she felt the hairs on her arms rise. "Bella, sweetie, is your imaginary friend standing over there in the corner right now?"

Bella slowly shook her head.

Jenn knew she wasn't going to get anywhere with these questions, especially at this time of night. So, she decided to let it go – for now. She would try to get to the bottom of it in the morning.

Jenn smiled at Bella and walked over to her bed to tuck her in. "OK. Now, try to get back to sleep, sweetie, and I'll see you in the morning. Goodnight, love you."

"Goodnight, Mummy. I love you."

As Jenn gently closed the door and turned off the landing light, she failed to notice the young woman with dark hair, dressed in white, standing behind her on the second step of the stairs.

The figure, who was watching Jenn intently, didn't appear sinister in the slightest. She simply looked lost, sad, and in need of a friend.

Jenn returned to bed and watched Bella on the monitor as she slowly drifted off to sleep.

Jenn, however, had a very restless night.

***

The next morning, Jenn sat at her dressing table, putting on her makeup while David got Olivia ready for nursery downstairs.

Bella was in the bathroom, brushing her teeth. She finished up, and was just about to head downstairs when Jenn called her.

"Bella, can you come here for a minute, sweetheart?"

Bella shuffled into the bedroom. "Yes, Mummy?" she asked.

Jenn put down her makeup, turned to Bella, and smiled. "Can you tell me who your imaginary friend is – the one you were talking to last night?" she asked gently.

Bella shrugged, her gaze dropping to the floor as she began to shuffle her feet. Clearly, she sensed she was about to get in trouble.

Jenn moved closer, her tone soft. "Bella, Mummy's not angry; you're not going to get in trouble for talking to your friend. Mummy just wants to know who they are." She paused, smiling softly. "You know, I had an imaginary friend when I was a little girl, too."

Bella looked up at her mum, her face lighting up with curiosity. "You did?" she asked. "What was their name?"

Jenn smiled warmly. "His name was Joey. He was a little talking kangaroo, about your height, and he always wore sunglasses!" she said, laughing at the memory.

Bella giggled. "A talking kangaroo? That's silly, Mummy! Kangaroos can't talk!"

Jenn chuckled too. "Well, my Joey could! He was my imaginary friend, and imaginary friends can do whatever you want them to!" she added with a playful wink.

"Well, my friend just looks normal," Bella said.

Jenn felt a wave of relief. *Good*, she thought. *She's starting to open up.* She often used this tactic with her young clients to help them feel more comfortable, and it seemed to be working with her daughter.

Jenn cleared her throat before asking, "So, what does your friend look like, sweetie? And when did you first meet her? Is it a her?"

Bella nodded. "She just turned up one day," she explained. "She's pretty, has dark hair, and she doesn't wear shoes."

"Aw, why doesn't she wear shoes?" Jenn asked, genuinely curious.

"Because she said she lost them a long time ago, Mummy."

"That's a shame," Jenn murmured.

Bella continued, "She looks sad sometimes. I think she just wants a friend, Mummy."

A lump formed in Jenn's throat. "Why is she sad, sweetheart?" she asked softly.

Bella shrugged, her gaze drifting.

Jenn smiled gently, trying to ease the tension. "OK, sweetie. Thanks for telling me about your friend. I hope she feels a little happier soon. Now, go and put your shoes on. I'll be down in a minute."

"OK, Mummy!" Bella said happily, bouncing towards the door.

As Bella left, a tear formed in Jenn's eye. She blinked it away, still feeling emotional.

But why? she thought. *Why am I feeling this way?*

Had a lonely, unhappy spirit really befriended Bella, or had she simply created an imaginary friend? Jenn didn't know, but suddenly, she was overwhelmed with grief and sadness for reasons she couldn't explain.

Shaking it off, Jenn quickly pulled herself together and finished putting on her makeup.

***

It was 2:47 am and Jenn was sleeping soundly on her right side, her left hand tucked under her pillow, supporting her chin, and her right arm outstretched with her palm resting over the mattress, facing the ceiling.

Suddenly, a small hand appeared and gently slipped into Jenn's relaxed palm.

Jenn jolted awake, gasping as she felt the child's tiny hand in hers. The room was pitch black, and she couldn't see anything.

The tiny hand released its grip, and Jenn heard soft footsteps on the carpet, running towards the end of the bed and out of the room.

"Olivia? Bella? Is that you?"

She expected to hear the kids' bedroom door open and close, but instead, the footsteps just stopped.

Quickly, Jenn checked the baby monitor – both girls were sleeping soundly in their beds.

With a mix of confusion and concern, Jenn threw the duvet off and got out of bed, heading towards the kids' room.

She turned on the landing light and opened the door. The room was now bathed in light, revealing both girls asleep in their beds.

Jenn opened the baby gate and crept closer to them, confirming they were both deep in sleep. Clearly, whatever Jenn had just experienced had nothing to do with the girls.

Was she dreaming? Or had she really felt a child's hand in hers?

She wasn't sure; all she knew for sure was that the experience had left her feeling more unsettled than ever.

Jenn quietly left the room and returned to her bed.

Needless to say, she didn't get much sleep for the rest of the night.

Chapter 8

One night, David was lying in bed, unable to sleep. His mind was racing, his body restless but exhausted. He couldn't stop thinking about all the recent strange happenings in the house.

He rolled over to face Jenn, who was sound asleep. David envied her. As soon as her head hit the pillow, she was out cold. He'd always said that Jenn was like a cat – she could fall asleep anywhere, at any time.

David rolled onto his back and glanced at his watch – it was 2:24 am. He sighed deeply. He and Jenn had gone to bed around 10 pm, and he had to get up with the kids at 6:30 am.

"Well, looks like I'm going to be shattered tomorrow," David muttered to himself as he hauled himself out of bed and headed downstairs to the kitchen. "I'm going to need a lot of coffee in the morning."

He cast his mind back to when he was a young boy. Whenever he couldn't sleep, Angela would give him some milk to help him drift off. That sounded pretty good right now.

He didn't bother turning on the kitchen light; an

ambient glow was spilling in through the windows from the streetlights outside.

David opened the fridge, squinting from the light that flooded out. It took a moment for his eyes to adjust.

As he bent down to grab the carton of milk, a dark figure appeared in the far corner of the room, silently watching him. David, however, was completely unaware. He unscrewed the cap of the milk carton and took a long gulp. The figure stood motionless, still staring, watching every move David made.

After a few moments, David stopped drinking and screwed the cap back on, placing the carton back on the shelf. As he rummaged around at the back of the fridge, a car passed by outside, its headlights sweeping across the room. For a brief moment, the light caught the figure standing in the corner, revealing its eyes, which glowed bright yellow like a cat's or a dog's.

Slowly, the figure's mouth opened and its eyes widened, growing even larger as they focused on David.

David heard the car passing and saw the headlights sweep across the room, sending a cold shiver down his spine. However, by the time he stood up and looked around, the car had passed and the room had returned to its familiar dark, still atmosphere. The figure remained in the shadows, but once again, David didn't notice it.

He turned his attention back to the fridge, pulling out a bag of salad from the back, now wilted and brown.

"Jesus, Jenn!" David muttered. *I don't know why she does that*, he thought, *buying bags of salad even though she never eats them.*

Rolling his eyes, he closed the fridge and walked over to the bin, tossing the rotten salad inside. He scanned the room for a moment before heading back upstairs, but the figure was gone.

***

The following night, Jenn was once again jolted awake by the sound of the baby monitor crackling into life. She checked the time – it was 1:38 am.

Bringing the monitor closer, her eyes adjusted to the dim light until she could see the screen. The kids were sleeping peacefully, but as her eyes adjusted further, shock and fear washed over her.

Standing over the children's beds was a dark, shadowy figure, moving slowly from one bed to the other, watching them sleep.

Jenn gasped loudly.

As the figure turned towards the camera, two glowing, reflective eyes stared back at her.

Jenn let out a terrified shriek, dropping the baby monitor.

She quickly threw off the duvet, her body propelled by pure adrenaline as her fight-or-flight instinct kicked in and she ran towards the kids' room. Like a lioness defending her own, she was ready to face it – whatever it was.

Jean reached the kids' bedroom door, unlocked the bifold baby gate, flicked on the landing light, and burst into the room.

The sudden flood of light startled the girls as the door flew open. Both Bella and Olivia sat up in bed, wide-eyed and confused as Jenn scanned the room. The noise and commotion had also woken David, who followed her into the room to investigate.

As the girls began to whimper, Jenn knelt down between their beds, her heart racing.

"What's wrong, Mummy? Why did you wake us up like that?" Bella asked.

David rubbed his eyes. "Yeah, Jenn, why did you wake them up like that?" he asked, his voice thick with sleep.

Jenn struggled to catch her breath, her chest tight as she hyperventilated, trying to calm herself down. "Mummy thought she saw something on the camera. I'm sorry – I didn't mean to startle you both."

David, trying to ease the tension, smiled and said, "I think Mummy was maybe having a silly dream and was sleepwalking… silly Mummy!"

Olivia giggled. "Silly Mummy, sleepwalking!" she repeated.

Jenn shot David a hard stare before turning back to the girls. "Yeah, Daddy's right. I think I was sleepwalking. Silly Mummy. Now, let's all get back to sleep, shall we? Goodnight, my little cherubs."

"Goodnight, Mummy!" they replied.

Jenn leaned down to kiss both girls on the head, tucking them in tightly. She then stood up and headed to the door, walking past David without even looking at him.

David smiled at the two girls. "Goodnight, kids. Sleep tight."

"Goodnight, Daddy!" they both replied as he closed the door. He then pulled the baby gate across, locked it, and headed back to bed.

In their bedroom, Jenn was sitting on the edge of the bed, still trying to steady her breathing.

David climbed back into bed and turned towards her. "What the hell was all that about, Jenn? You pretty much scared the crap out of them!"

Jenn cleared her throat and took a sip of water from the bottle beside her. "It's nothing. Just leave it."

David frowned. "Leave what? Clearly, something got you spooked. I just want to know what happened."

Jenn turned to face David, frustration flickering in her eyes. "Would you really believe me if I told you?" she snapped.

David opened his mouth to answer, but Jenn cut him off.

"What if I told you I saw something strange – like a shadowy figure, standing over the kids, on the monitor? Would you believe me then, David?"

He lowered his head, sighing deeply.

Jenn scoffed. "Yup, just what I thought. So, like I said, let's just leave it and try to get some sleep."

They both lay there in silence, the awkward tension hanging heavy between them, until David finally drifted off to sleep.

It took hours for Jenn to find any rest. All she could think about was what she'd seen on the monitor – those reflective eyes.

***

David's alarm jingle blared at 6:30 am, pulling him out of a groggy sleep. He sleepily reached over, switched it off, and swung his legs out of bed. Rubbing his eyes and yawning, he glanced at Jenn, who was still fast asleep, snoring loudly. David smiled – Jenn had never been a morning person.

He reached for his phone and saw a notification from the CCTV system's app. The message read: *Movement Detected @ 3:33 am.* David clicked on the notification, which opened the app and brought up the recorded clip.

He sat up and watched the video intently.

The clip showed what appeared to be a young woman dressed in an old hospital gown, her long dark hair cascading over her left shoulder. With her head slightly cocked to the left, she walked slowly into view from behind the garage, pausing with her back to the camera.

David's heart began to race; he couldn't believe what he was seeing.

The woman turned around, locking eyes with the camera for a few moments and making David's blood run cold.

He brought the phone closer to his face, and just as he did, the woman let out a blood-curdling scream before the camera went blank.

David jumped in shock, dropping the phone on the covers. Then, snatching it up, he continued to watch the video. The camera was working again, but now, the girl was gone.

He replayed the clip, slowing it down to watch it frame by frame. He reached the part where the woman screamed, just before the camera went blank, and it looked like her face was just inches from the lens. In the final frames, it seemed like she went from standing to somehow leaping directly at the camera – but how could that be? The camera was positioned about eight and a half feet off the ground!

David paused the video before it cut out, staring at the image of the young woman. She appeared to be around 18 or 19, with pale, dirty-looking skin and brown eyes. But what struck him the most was the expression of sheer distress on her face.

Who is this girl? David wondered. *Where did she come from?*

She must have entered through the back garden; if she had come in the front, the exterior camera would have picked her up as she entered the driveway.

But more troubling still – *Where did she go?*

***

It was the weekend again, and David had gone to visit his mum to help with a few DIY jobs she'd asked him to do.

Jenn and the kids were at home. Jenn was doing her usual cleaning and tidying in the kitchen, while the kids sat quietly at the table, drawing pictures. Once Jenn had finished in the kitchen, she walked over to the table to check on the girls.

"You two are awfully quiet today," Jenn said with a smile. "I'm not used to it."

She got a grunt in response.

Jenn picked up the small pile of pictures the kids had drawn and began studying each one. The first picture was full of doodles – various things like cats, dogs, rabbits, and flowers. The next drawing was of David, Jenn, and the two girls standing in front of what appeared to be their house. They were all smiling, and the words 'My Family' had been written at the top.

Jenn smiled – until something in the picture caught her eye. There, in the attic skylight window, was a dark, featureless figure. Jenn's smile slowly faded.

She turned to the next picture and gasped. It showed the two girls standing in their room, holding hands with a horrifying figure – dressed in black, with red and yellow eyes.

Jenn looked at the girls, who were still busy drawing, then glanced down at another picture. This one looked similar to the last, but she could tell Olivia had drawn it as it wasn't as detailed; the man in this picture was simply a black scribble with two arms, holding hands with the kids.

Jenn cleared her throat. "Girls… who drew this picture?" she asked softly.

The girls didn't answer.

"Bella? Olivia? Mummy's trying to talk to you…"

The girls stopped what they were doing and looked up.

"Yes, Mummy?" Bella asked.

"Who drew these pictures?" Jenn asked again, holding them up for the girls to see.

"I drew these two," Bella said, pointing at the more detailed ones, "and Olivia drew this one…"

"Yes, I drew that one," Olivia said proudly.

Jenn paused for a moment. "Well, Mummy thinks they're very good… but I was wondering, can you tell me who this is?" She pointed at the shadowy figure. "I remember you drew a similar picture to this a while ago."

They both shrugged.

"Is it your little friend, Andy?" Jenn asked.

"No," they both replied.

"Is it an imaginary friend?"

"No…"

"Well, it must be someone…" Jenn pressed.

"It's the Black Finger Man, Mummy!" Olivia said, matter-of-factly.

"Olivia, shhh!" Bella hissed. "You're not supposed to tell!"

Olivia quickly put her hands up to her mouth and giggled.

A wave of fear washed over Jenn. "Bella, why wasn't your sister meant to tell me? Who is that? Who is the Black Finger Man?"

Bella shrugged. "I don't know, Mummy…" She then picked up one of her pencils and went back to drawing her picture.

Jenn's stomach was churning. An uneasy feeling had settled in, and all kinds of thoughts were racing through her mind. Who was this mysterious man? Was he somehow involved in all the strange things happening around the house? Why was he called the Black Finger Man? Was he grooming her children?!

Jenn's frustration started to build as she grabbed the pencil from her daughter's hand. "Bella!" she shouted.

Bella froze, startled.

"Look at me!" Jenn demanded, raising her voice. "This is important!"

Bella met her mum's eyes.

"Now, tell me who this person is right now! And where did you meet him?"

Bella's eyes filled with tears, and she began to cry.

"I... I don't know," she sobbed. "He was in my dream a few weeks ago, and I just started drawing him..."

"So, he's not a real person?"

"No!"

"Then why is your little sister drawing him too?" she pressed.

"Because I told her about my dream, and she saw my picture and copied me!"

Jenn felt a wave of relief wash over her, but it was quickly followed by a tinge of guilt for making Bella cry. She knelt down to Bella's level and gently wiped her tears away. "Look, sweetheart, I'm sorry for shouting at you," Jenn said softly. "I just wanted to know who it was in the picture. Remember how Mummy and Daddy are always telling you and your sister about stranger danger?"

Bella nodded.

"Well, Mummy was just getting a bit worried, that's all. OK? Mummy and Daddy just want to keep you and your sister safe."

Bella nodded again as Jenn pulled her into a hug.

At the same time, Olivia jumped off her chair and rushed over to give Bella a hug too. "It's OK, Bella... Mummy didn't mean to shout," Olivia said kindly, as Jenn smiled.

"Now, why don't you both go out and play in the garden? It's a nice day," Jenn suggested.

"OK, Mummy," they both replied, heading towards the back door and running out into the garden.

Jenn picked up the drawings and studied them again, her mind racing. She decided she was going to show these to David – at some point. She knew he would dismiss her concerns, as usual, but she didn't care. There was something off about this house, she just knew it.

She took the drawings into the front living room and placed them on the floating shelf near the chimney breast for safekeeping.

Later that afternoon, David returned home. The girls were sitting on the couch, engrossed in their iPads.

"Hi girls!" David said cheerily.

The girls barely acknowledged him, grunting in response; they were far too absorbed in their YouTube videos.

David rolled his eyes and went to the kitchen to put the kettle on, just as Jenn came down the stairs.

David smiled at Jenn as she walked in. "Hi babe, how are you? Fancy a cup of tea? I've just put the kettle on."

Jenn shook her head, a concerned look on her face. "No thanks," she replied. "David, can I talk to you in the other room for a minute? I've got something to show you."

"Sure," he said, sensing something was troubling her. He followed her into the front living room. "Are you OK, sweetheart? What's wrong?" he asked.

Jenn walked over to the shelf and picked up the kids' drawings. "David," she began, "the kids have been drawing some really disturbing pictures recently. And before you dismiss me – like you always do – I want you to take a good, hard look at them and tell me what you make of them."

David sighed, rubbed his face, and switched to his usual humouring mode. "OK, Jenn. No problem," he said with a smile, trying to lighten the mood.

Jenn handed him the drawings, and David's expression shifted as he looked at them. His face slowly dropped, the hairs on the back of his neck stood up, and a knot began to tighten in his stomach.

Jenn studied his face intently. She could see that he didn't know how to react.

After a few moments, David cleared his throat. "What are these, Jenn?" he asked, his voice quieter now.

"I don't know, David," she replied. "I was hoping you could give me your opinion. The girls said this is the Black Finger Man."

David looked up from the drawings, stunned. "The Black Finger Man?" he repeated, disbelief evident in his voice.

"Yes... Bella said he visits her in her dreams," Jenn explained.

David scoffed. "Well, there you go. He's clearly an imaginary friend, and they're just drawing him."

"For Christ's sake, David!" Jenn snapped, her frustration bubbling over. "When are you going to wake the fuck up and realise there's something going on in this house?! And now it's beginning to affect our children!"

David sighed, rubbing his eyes. "Jenn, calm down."

"Don't tell me to calm down, David! You clearly don't think these drawings are normal – I watched your face drop when you looked at them!"

David shifted uncomfortably, trying to find the right words. "I'll admit, they're a bit strange and creepy, but I don't think there's anything to be concerned about, Jenn."

"Nothing to be concerned about?!" she snapped, tapping the pages aggressively. "David, when kids draw their imaginary friends, they're usually happy drawings, fun scenes… they don't draw dark, sinister figures like these!"

David looked at the drawing of the creepy figure standing in the attic. "I hear what you're saying, Jenn, and I'm not saying you're wrong. All *I'm* saying is that it boils down to a matter of opinion, and in my opinion, there's nothing to worry about here. The kids are happy and healthy – they're just expressing themselves."

Jenn stood there, staring at him for a few moments before rubbing her face and letting out a heavy sigh. "You know what, David?" she said, the exhaustion evident in her voice. "I just can't deal with you sometimes. Your problem is, you never know when to admit you're wrong." With that, she snatched the drawings from his hands before storming out of the room and slamming the door behind her.

David just stood there, frozen, processing her words.

Meanwhile, Jenn walked into the kitchen, took a deep breath, and looked at the drawings for a moment before placing them in the cupboard above the kettle.

Back in the living room, David closed his eyes, rubbed his temples, and sighed.

Chapter 9

David was visiting a patient for work. Gustavo Liberman – or Gus, as he preferred to be called. Gus was one of David's favourite patients, having built a close rapport with him and his wife, Adina – or Ina, as she liked to be called.

Gus was a well-dressed, intelligent old gentleman, always clean-shaven, drenched in Old Spice, and with never a hair out of place. He and Ina, an elderly Jewish couple, had been together since they were young.

When David first visited them for Gus's initial physiotherapy assessment, they were so kind and welcoming, asking lots of questions and even wondering if David was Jewish because of his name. In fact, they kept him chatting for nearly two hours, but David didn't mind; it was one of the things he loved about his job, meeting people and building relationships with his patients and their families.

Gus and Ina had never had children of their own. They had tried for many years, but unfortunately, it never happened for them. It was a shame, David often thought, as they would have made wonderful parents and even better grandparents.

Every time David came to visit, they would ask after the kids and eagerly look at any new pictures he had on his phone. Ina would always pick up a packet of sweets for them whenever she went shopping, insisting that David take them home with him.

Gus had recently suffered a fall and fractured his hip, and after being discharged from the hospital, a hospital bed had been set up in their living room. David's job was to help Gus regain his strength and confidence through exercises, stretches, and reaching personal goals – one of which was to walk up the stairs and sleep in his own bed again.

Today, when David arrived at Gus's house, something felt wrong. As he walked up the garden path, he could hear screaming and shouting coming from inside. Concerned, he rang the doorbell, and Ina answered almost instantly. She looked exhausted, pale, and distressed.

"Oh, David, thank God you're here!" she exclaimed. "I think Gus has got an infection, and he's hallucinating. I've been up all night with him, and I've called the doctor several times."

David placed a hand on her shoulder. "It's OK, Ina. Try and calm down. I'll go in and see him. Has he had anything to drink in the past 24 hours?"

Ina shook her head. "No, I can't get him to drink anything," she replied. "He just keeps screaming and shouting, then he wears himself out and falls asleep for about twenty minutes. Then it starts all over again."

"OK," David said gently, "not to worry – he

probably has a urine infection from being dehydrated. I'll call the doctor after I've seen him. Why don't you go into the kitchen, make yourself a cup of tea, and sit down for five minutes? I'm here now, and I'm not going anywhere until I know you and Gus are OK."

Ina touched David's face, her eyes shining with gratitude. "Thank you, David. You're a good boy."

David smiled as she turned and walked down the hallway to the kitchen. He then opened the old-fashioned 1970s frosted glass door to the living room, where Gus was lying in bed, shouting, speaking in broken sentences, and occasionally slipping into Yiddish. He looked pale, tired, and unkempt, his forehead saturated with sweat. It was clear that the infection had been affecting him for days now.

When Gus saw David, his face lit up. "David! My boy! I'm so glad to see you! They're coming… they're coming here to kill us… we need to get out of here…"

At least he recognises me, David thought. *That's a good sign.*

"Gus," David said gently, "it's OK, my friend. You're at home, and you're safe. I promise."

Gus grew more agitated, his eyes wide with fear. "No, David! Trust me, they're coming! We need to go… we need to go now!"

"Who's coming to get us, Gus?" David asked patiently, trying to stay calm.

Gus sat up in bed, falling silent, and then looked around the room as if checking there was no one about to hear him. "I can't tell you that just yet, my boy," he whispered, his eyes still darting around the living room, "but trust me, when the time is right, I will."

David knew he wasn't going to get anywhere trying to reassure him, so he decided to shift the conversation to something lighter. He took out his phone and began to show Gus the latest pictures of the kids. "Look at this, Gus," David said, handing him his phone with a photo of Olivia and Bella on the screen. "I took this at the weekend while we were at the park."

Gus stared at the screen, smiling despite himself. "Ah, look at them. They're little angels."

"Keep flicking through them, Gus – there are loads of pictures on there," David told him. "While you're looking through them, do you mind if I take your blood pressure and temperature?"

Gus – who was now engrossed in looking at the pictures – had calmed down and was only half listening to David. "Yes, of course, my boy. Do whatever you need to do," he replied absentmindedly.

In David's line of work, he had learnt that showing distressed or agitated patients pictures of pets, animals, or children could help calm them down and defuse nearly any situation.

While Gus was occupied with the phone, David reached into his backpack, pulled out his blood pressure monitor, and slid Gus's arm through the cuff, adjusting it to the correct size before pressing the start button. The machine beeped, and the automatic pump began inflating the cuff. Meanwhile, David retrieved his handheld contactless temperature gun and pulse monitor from his bag. He attached the pulse monitor to Gus's right index finger and turned the temperature gun on, holding it in front of Gus's forehead.

The temperature gun beeped, the digital screen displaying 39.5°C. The oxygen monitor showed that Gus's oxygen saturation levels were at 92%, and his blood pressure was 159/112, which wasn't a good sign. It was clear that Gus had an infection and needed urgent medical attention.

David looked up at Gus, who was still happily flicking through the pictures on the phone. Shaking his head, David pulled a packet of antibacterial wipes from his bag, carefully removing the equipment from Gus and sanitising it thoroughly.

Once he'd put all of his equipment back into the bag, he glanced at Gus, who was now exploring David's phone, pressing various buttons, tapping in and out of apps, flicking, and swiping.

"Gus… Gus?" David said softly, gently touching Gus's arm.

"Hmm?" Gus replied, still absorbed in the phone, almost in a trance-like state. This wasn't necessarily a bad thing, David thought. At least Gus wasn't agitated or distressed.

David spoke a little louder to get Gus's attention. "Gus, you have an infection at the moment, and your temperature is really high. So, I'm going to call the doctor and see if we can get you admitted to hospital – you'll need some intravenous fluids and antibiotics. OK?"

At this point, Gus looked up from the phone, still with a soft smile on his face. However, it quickly vanished when he saw David; he started screaming hysterically and talking in Yiddish, dropping David's phone in the process. He then raised his arm and pointed directly at David. "Golem! Golem!" he shouted.

David – who could see the terror in Gus's eyes – tried to calm him down, but it only seemed to frighten Gus more.

Gus jumped away from David, still pointing and shouting things in Yiddish – things David couldn't understand.

At that moment, Ina hurried through from the kitchen. "What's happening, David?" she asked, distraught. "I thought you'd calmed him down!"

David turned to her, looking worried. "He was calm! I showed him some pictures of the kids while I took his temperature and blood pressure. Then, I told him he had an infection and would need to go to the hospital. That's when he started to get agitated again."

Ina started speaking Yiddish to Gus, trying to soothe him. She wore a confused expression on her face as David picked up words like 'Golem' and his own name.

"What is he saying, Ina?" David asked, his concern growing.

Ina turned to him, still looking bewildered. "He is saying you're a Golem… a demon of sorts. He's very confused," she replied.

David picked up his phone and backpack from the floor and walked to the hallway, taking a moment to turn back to Gus. "Don't worry, Gus, you'll be OK," he reassured him. "It's just an infection. We'll get you to the hospital and get you better."

Gus didn't take his eyes off David, still shouting

'Golem' along with broken sentences in Yiddish.

Ina followed David out into the hallway. "I'm sorry, David. He obviously doesn't mean it; he's just very confused."

David smiled, trying to ease her worries. "Don't worry about it, Ina. That was nothing. When I did my rotation on the wards, I used to get bedpans of urine thrown at me... and that was just from my colleagues!"

Ina chuckled.

It was nice to see her smile, David thought. Even if just for a moment.

"So," David continued. "you were right, Ina. He has got an infection. His temperature is 39.5, his oxygen saturation levels are at 92%, and his blood pressure is 159/112."

"Oh my God," Ina said, putting her hand up to her mouth.

"I know, Ina, but don't worry. I'm going to call the doctor right now and ask him to send an ambulance. I'll be sitting in my car if you need me, and I'll wait there until they arrive, OK?"

Ina nodded, though she was shaking a little. "OK, David. Thank you, you're a good boy."

David smiled, let himself out of the house, and started walking towards his car. As he opened his phone, he noticed the voice recorder app was open – and it was recording. Gus must have pressed it while he was playing with the phone.

David quickly pressed stop, swiped out of the app, and returned to the home screen. Then, just as he reached his car, he hit the big green telephone button to make a call. Climbing into the driver's seat, he scrolled through his contacts and called the doctor's surgery. He gave the receptionist a detailed description of Gus's symptoms and requested that the doctor urgently send an ambulance.

Once the call was done, David pulled out his laptop and started updating Gus's notes.

About ten minutes later, the doctor called back. David explained Gus's symptoms and observations to the doctor, who confirmed that he would send an ambulance. David advised the doctor that he was more than happy to wait until they arrived so he could give the medical handover.

After hanging up, David finished typing his notes and documented everything he'd just discussed with the doctor.

He glanced at the digital clock on his laptop: 1:43 pm. Nearly coffee time, he thought. He closed his laptop, slipped it into his bag, and grabbed his phone to send Jenn a text.

As he picked up his phone, he noticed a notification from the voice recorder app, alerting him that a new voice note had been recorded. David tapped the notification, which opened the app and started to play the recording. It was his voice, from when he was in the house with Gus.

"Gus, you have an infection at the moment, and your temperature is really high. So, I'm going to call the doctor and see if we can get you admitted to hospital – you'll need some intravenous fluids and antibiotics. OK?"

David was about to stop the recording when he

heard Gus shouting. But then, amidst Gus's screams, another voice cut through – one thick with a German accent.

"Juden... juden... I will take your soul, juden... Golem! Golem! Yes, juden, I am..."

Then, the sinister voice began to laugh, taunting Gus even more.

David sat in shock for several moments, and then listened to the recording again.

Who is the other voice? he pondered, his mind racing.

A tap on the driver's side window suddenly jolted David back to reality. Startled, he stopped the recording and looked over. It was Ina, standing by the car door, smiling and holding what looked like a cup of coffee.

David smiled and wound down the window.

"I thought you could do with a cup, sweetheart," Ina said as she passed the coffee through the window. "Gus is asleep now."

"Thanks, Ina," David replied, taking the drink. "It's good he's asleep. I've updated the doctor, and the ambulance is on its way. It shouldn't be too long. Why don't you go and rest? I'll wait here for them and give them an update."

Ina smiled. "Thank you, sweetheart. You're a good boy," she said, before turning away.

"Ina, before you go, just a quick question," David said quickly, before she walked off.

"Yes, love?" she replied, coming back to the car window.

"What does 'juden' mean?"

Ina frowned. "Juden? It means 'Jew' in German. Why?"

"Oh, no reason," David replied. "Gus was shouting it before you came into the living room earlier, and I'd never heard it before."

Ina smiled, laughing a little. "You have a good, strong Jewish name, and you didn't know what juden meant? Oh, David, you're funny. Even on the darkest days, you always make me laugh."

David smiled sheepishly as he watched Ina walk away and into the house. He didn't know what to make of what he'd heard on the recording, but it had unsettled him deeply.

That week, David kept a close eye on Gus's progress while he was in hospital, using TrakCare – a system for healthcare staff to monitor patients. Unfortunately, the medical team couldn't get Gus's infection under control. He went into cardiac arrest and, tragically, passed away.

A few days later, David called Ina to offer his condolences and to ask when the funeral would be, as he wanted to pay his respects to Gus. After all, he had a lot of time and respect for Gus and Ina. She told him it was the following week.

David attended the funeral, and it was a deeply sad day. This was always the hardest part of his job – when a patient he'd built a strong rapport with passed away.

***

One Friday afternoon, David arrived at the office after a patient visit and made his way to his desk. He dumped his backpack onto the desk, pulled out his chair, and collapsed into it with a loud, tired sigh.

Matt, one of David's colleagues, emerged from the

kitchen with a cup of coffee. Matt was a newly qualified physiotherapist, a nice lad in his twenties. He was tall, with blond hair and blue eyes, and a total gym fanatic. Well-built, with broad shoulders and muscles everywhere, he'd worked as a personal trainer while studying to be a physiotherapist.

David liked him. Matt reminded him of himself at that age – enthusiastic, always eager to learn, and most importantly, he had a knack for connecting with his patients.

"Hello, mate," Matt greeted him. "I didn't hear you come in. Do you fancy a coffee?"

David looked up and smiled. "Hi, Matt. I'll get one in a minute, thanks – I just need to catch my breath first."

Matt smiled. "Hard day?" he asked. "You look knackered."

David rubbed his eyes . "No, not really. I'm just knackered in general these days."

"How come?" Matt asked.

David sighed. "Well, I've got a pretty heavy caseload at the moment," he explained, "but the main thing is, since we moved into the new house, there's been a lot of strange stuff happening. Jenn and the kids are getting really freaked out by it."

Matt frowned. "What kind of strange stuff?"

David cleared his throat. "Just odd things – stuff getting moved around or broken, knocking on walls and doors, light switches clicking on and off at all hours of the night but no lights actually coming on…"

Matt scratched his cheek. "Sounds like you have a

visitor. Have you cleansed the house with sage since you moved in?"

David rolled his eyes, chuckling. "Oh, don't tell me you're into all that too? You sound just like my mum!"

"The paranormal and supernatural? Absolutely!" Matt replied enthusiastically. "I also believe in UFOs, aliens, Bigfoot, time travel… pretty much every conspiracy theory out there."

David sighed. "OK," he said, grinning, "try and convince me. Make me believe!"

Matt cleared his throat. "Well… from what you're telling me, it sounds like there's some kind of presence in your house. It's not uncommon, really. Usually, it's just an average spirit passing through…"

David frowned in confusion. "Right… go on," he said, intrigued.

"These spirits can be playful and mischievous at times," Matt continued, "moving things around, knocking on walls, that sort of thing. The easiest way to get rid of them is to simply ask them to go away and move on."

David grinned.

Matt held up a hand. "I know what you're thinking, David, but hear me out."

David nodded. "Please continue," he said.

"OK," Matt replied. "Once you've asked it to leave, you sage and cleanse the house. Hopefully, that should be the end of it. However, if that doesn't work, you're probably dealing with something else entirely."

"Something else? What do you mean?" David asked, intrigued despite himself.

Matt paused, gathering his thoughts. "Well, you get

different types of spirits and presences. The most common is the one I just described. Then, there are the more mischievous ones, who go out of their way to disrupt your life. They do things like mimic the people they're tormenting." He paused again, taking a deep breath before continuing. "Then, finally, there's the more sinister type of entity. This one will physically make its presence known. It might move furniture around, throw things, and so on, and that's what is known as a poltergeist. These things are pure evil, with demonic tendencies. Their only desire is to possess the living they've targeted…"

David's grin slowly faded, replaced by a look of concern.

Noticing the shift in David's demeanour, Matt asked, "Has something like that happened at home?"

David cleared his throat. "Well, the kids have been drawing these really strange pictures recently – of someone they call the Black Finger Man – who visits them at night. And Olivia even claimed to see a man in the garden."

Matt's expression grew serious.

"But surely that's just their imagination running wild, right?" David asked, his voice tinged with desperation. "I mean, that's what kids do, isn't it? Make up stories and imaginary friends?"

Matt nodded slowly. "Yes, of course. That's how children develop their personalities and social skills… but research has shown that children are more sensitive to the supernatural than adults. They can see things we can't. Tell me, what time do these things usually happen?"

"Umm, usually between two and three in the

morning, I think," David replied. "Why does that matter?"

Matt cleared his throat again. "Because there's something called the witching hour, or the Devil's hour. It's when supernatural entities are most active. It's usually between midnight and 4 am."

David listened intently, rubbing his chin. "OK… you've got my attention. I'll get my mum to cleanse the house as soon as possible."

Matt nodded in agreement. "If I were you, mate, I'd also get some holy water and iron shavings."

David raised his eyebrows. "Holy water? Matt, we're not a religious family… and what are the iron shavings for?"

"You don't need to be religious for these things to be useful," Matt explained. "If this entity has attached itself to you, sooner or later, it will manifest into a full-blown apparition. So, you'll need to be prepared to protect yourself. Iron shavings and holy water are like acid to these things." He noticed David's worried expression. "Don't worry – it probably won't come to that, but it's better to hope for the best and prepare for the worst. The best advice I can give you is to never show fear to this thing, because paranormal entities feed on fear. And, whatever you do, don't try to bargain with it. Doing that would be like formally inviting it into your life. Have you ever heard the saying 'never make a deal with the Devil'?"

David nodded.

"It comes from the myth of a German magician and chemist, Dr Johann Georg Faust, who sold his soul to the Devil in exchange for his powers back in the 15th century… You should look it up."

David stood up from his chair, slowly digesting everything he'd just heard. "Well, Matt, you've certainly given me a lot to think about," he said with a smile. "I'll keep you posted on my ghoulish house guest. For now, I need to get back to the real world; I'm going to make a coffee and type up my notes."

David was on his way to the kitchen when he suddenly stopped and turned around, a big grin on his face. "You know, Matt, if your physiotherapy career ever goes tits up, you could always become a Ghostbuster."

Matt looked up from his computer and laughed.

***

It was Friday night – the night David's mum, Angela, would often take the kids to her house for a sleepover. The kids loved staying at their granny's house, and it gave David and Jenn the opportunity to spend some quality time together.

This night, however, Jenn had promised her mum she'd go to bingo with her, which suited David perfectly. He had a nice, quiet evening planned.

He was going to run a hot jacuzzi bath and soak for an hour or so with a couple of cold beers. Then, when he was finished, he was going to order an Indian takeaway and settle in front of the TV – with a few more beers – to watch the films he enjoyed. Action movies, gangster flicks, and sci-fi films. Jenn, of course, would have called them 'crap,' as she preferred rom-coms and chick flicks. So, David was relishing the idea of his evening alone.

Angela had picked up the kids from school, and Jenn had left not long before. It was time.

David started running the jacuzzi bath, the water piping hot. His muscles ached, likely due to his recent demanding caseload of patients – or perhaps from the stress of worrying about Jenn and her persistent cough, or the strange happenings in the house. He had a feeling it was a combination of all three.

He tested the water, adding a bit of cold and getting it to the perfect temperature. Then, after stripping off, he was just about to step into the bath when it hit him: He'd forgotten the most important thing… the beer!

He slipped his bathrobe back on, tied it at his waist, and made his way downstairs to the kitchen. He opened the drawer for the bottle opener, grabbed two beers from the fridge, and was about to close the door when he paused, before grabbing another beer for good measure. Why not? After all, it wasn't every day he got to enjoy a quiet night alone.

With that, David marched back upstairs, opened one of the beers, took a long satisfying gulp, and set all three bottles on the closed toilet seat lid.

Then, after hanging his bathrobe over the hook on the bathroom door, he slowly slipped into the warm water, letting out a contented sigh. He took a deep breath, submerged his head and body under the water for a few seconds, then resurfaced, stretching his body as nearly all of his joints cracked. Once again, he let out a satisfied sigh.

David picked up his open bottle of beer and turned on the jacuzzi, the jets firing hot streams of bubbles into every part of his body. He took another sip, closed his eyes, and let out a deep breath. Before he knew it, the bottle was empty, and he was feeling completely relaxed.

After a few moments, his relaxation was interrupted by the sound of something coming from downstairs.

"David?... David?... Are you there?"

It sounded like Jenn calling him.

"Jenn? Is that you?" he shouted over the sound of the jacuzzi jets. "I'm in the bath!"

"David?... David?... Are you there?"

"Jesus Christ," he muttered, annoyed now. "I'm in the bath, Jenn! What is it? And what are you doing back? I thought you went to bingo?"

Suddenly, David heard the sound of footsteps slowly walking across the laminate flooring in the box room. He quickly turned off the jets, cocked his head, and listened.

The footsteps slowly made their way to the bathroom door and then stopped. David could just make out the shadow of two feet under the door.

"Jenn? Is that you?" he called, his voice cracking.

There was no answer. Instead, all that followed were three loud knocks on the bathroom door.

Thud... thud... thud....

David jumped, his heart racing as panic set in.

"Jenn... if that's you... it's not funny anymore! You're really starting to freak me out!" he yelled.

Still, there was no answer.

David's heart continued to race as his eyes remained fixed on the shadowy feet beneath the door. Then, the feet suddenly turned to the left and vanished.

That's when David's fight-or-flight response kicked

in. Leaping out of the bath, he grabbed his bathrobe from the door and quickly put it on. Empty beer bottle still in hand, he opened the bathroom door and raised the bottle above his head, ready to confront the intruder on the other side.

When he opened the door and stepped into the hallway, however, there was no one there.

"Hello? Who's there?" he called out as he checked all of the upstairs rooms before descending the stairs. Reaching the bottom, he found the house eerily quiet. He checked every room, window, and door in the house. There was no one. Everything was locked.

With his pulse still racing, David rushed back upstairs to grab his phone from the bedroom. He needed to call Jenn.

She picked up after four rings. "Hey babe, what's up?" she asked. "Our game's just about to start."

"Were you just in the house a minute ago?" he asked, trying to keep his voice steady.

"In the house? No, Mum and I are at bingo, remember? Why?"

David didn't want to alarm her, so he decided to tell a little white lie. "Oh, nothing, sweetheart. I must be hearing things," he said, trying to sound casual. "Anyway, have a great time, and good luck – I hope you win. Love you, bye."

Jenn giggled. "OK, love you too. Bye."

David hung up, his mind reeling. He was shaken to his core. Was he going mad? Had he really heard Jenn calling out to him?

He could dismiss that, but what had really freaked

him out were the footsteps, the shadows of the feet, and the knocking. He knew he hadn't imagined those.

One thing was for sure – David's quiet, relaxing night had well and truly gone out the window.

Chapter 10

David's car was due for its MOT in a couple of weeks, so he decided to spend Saturday afternoon checking it over to save on garage costs. He needed to change the oil, replace a couple of bulbs, and give it a general clear-out – something he'd been putting off for months. With two young kids, the back seats and footwells had turned into a germy nest of crumbs, crisp packets, sweet wrappers, and toys. It was a mess.

Meanwhile, Jenn and the kids were inside. Jenn was going through her usual cleaning and tidying routine while the kids, unusually quiet, were sitting on the couch watching their iPads.

Jenn was over at the kids' art corner, gathering up scrap bits of paper and random drawings. One in particular caught her eye.

It was similar to the one Bella had drawn weeks ago, with the four of them standing in the garden in front of the house. This one, however, was different – there was no sinister Black Finger Man in sight.

Studying the picture for a moment, Jenn could tell that Bella had drawn it. It depicted the house with David,

Jenn, and the kids standing together and smiling in the garden on a sunny day. But, at the side of the house, there were two other figures with sad faces – one was a little boy, who appeared to be crying, and the other was a girl or a woman in a white dress who had her arm around him. What concerned Jenn the most, however, were the many dark, sad faces that appeared to be looking out from the attic skylight window.

Jenn glanced over at Bella, who was staring intently at her iPad watching YouTube videos, smiling and giggling every now and then. Jenn knew she needed to try a different approach to find out why Bella kept drawing these strange pictures. So, she walked over to the couch and sat next to her daughter.

"Bella, sweetie, can you pause the video for a minute?" Jenn said gently. "Mummy needs to ask you something."

Bella looked up at her mum and did as she was told. "Yes, Mummy?"

Jenn gave her a big smile. "This is a lovely drawing," she said, holding out the piece of paper, "did you draw it?"

Bella smiled and nodded.

"Can you tell Mummy what we're all doing in this drawing?" Jenn asked.

"We're playing in the front garden on a hot sunny day!" Bella said proudly.

Jenn smiled. "I can see that, it looks like we're all having fun! But Bella, who is that little boy? He looks so sad," she added, pointing at him.

"That's Andy, Mummy. He gets sad sometimes."

"Ah, Andy," said Jenn. "Why is he sad, sweetie?"

"Because he can't find his mummy."

Jenn paused for a moment. "That's not good, is it? Where is Andy's mummy, Bella?"

Bella just shrugged.

Jenn cleared her throat slightly before continuing. "OK, and who is this with Andy? Is that not his mummy?"

Bella shook her head. "No, that's Andy's friend," she explained.

"Oh, I see… What's her name?" Jenn asked.

Bella shrugged again. "I don't know, Mummy. She comes to get Andy sometimes when he plays with us."

"Is she maybe his big sister?" Jenn asked, curious.

Bella shook her head. "No, she's just his friend. I thought she was his sister at first, but Andy said, 'Definitely not my sister.'"

"Ah, OK, sweetie. So, last question, then I'll let you get back to your iPad. Who are these sad-looking people in the attic?" Jenn asked, pointing at the windows in the picture.

"I don't know, Mummy… I just had a feeling they were sad, so I drew them."

Jenn smiled. She didn't want Bella to feel she was being interrogated, so she decided to leave it at that. "OK, sweetie. Thank you for telling me about your lovely drawing."

Bella looked up, smiling at her mum, then returned to her iPad. Jenn smiled back and kissed Bella on the head before getting up from the couch and heading into the kitchen.

As she walked, Jenn felt a tightness in her stomach. Her instincts were screaming at her to tell David about the drawings and share her concerns, but part of her hesitated. After all, was there even any point? The last time she'd shown him the kids' creepy drawings, he'd made her feel like she was wasting her breath.

So, instead, she folded the drawing and slid it into the kitchen unit above the kettle, alongside the others.

***

A few months before the house move, David had injured his back while working with a patient. At the time, his line manager had referred him to occupational health. As a physiotherapist, David knew this was a waste of time – a mere box-ticking exercise his line manager had to complete to cover herself. That particular day, he had a follow-up appointment with occupational health to assess how he was doing and whether he could still carry out his duties.

The occupational health department was located in a very old hospital on the other side of the city. Built in the 1800s, it was no longer a functioning hospital. All of the old wards had been repurposed into day clinics or various other departments. The decor was outdated and tired, almost like stepping back in time to the 1980s. The walls, once a clinical white, had faded into a yellowish cream, while the heavy pine doors and doorframes, thick with layers of varnish, had turned dark brown, adding to the building's aged feel. Everything in the building looked old and worn.

As David walked down the corridor, he passed an old

payphone – its bubble hood a relic from the past – before entering reception. Once there, he headed straight for the lifts and pressed the button. It took a while for the lift to spring to life, but eventually, he heard a metallic clunk and a lot of rattling coming from above.

David rolled his eyes. This was just typical of the NHS – they never wanted to spend money on anything and were always cutting corners.

The lift doors finally opened and David stepped in, pressing the button for the sixth floor.

A second later, the lift's robotic voice crackled into life. "Ground floor… Mind the doors… Doors closing… Going up…"

The doors shut, and the lift began its ascent. David tutted, rolling his eyes again as the lift lights flickered on and off. The lift rattled and clunked its way up the shaft, then suddenly stopped.

"Please… wait…" the robotic voice announced.

David sighed. "Well, it's not like I can go anywhere, is it?" he complained out loud. "Stupid lift… Come on!" he muttered, pressing the sixth-floor button repeatedly.

The robotic voice crackled back to life. "Going up… Sixth floor…"

David huffed as the lift jerked into motion, eventually reaching his floor.

He stepped out and walked around the corner to the occupational health department. After identifying himself to the receptionist, she gestured for him to take a seat in the empty, dated waiting area. Fortunately, he didn't have to wait long before he was escorted into an old treatment room that had been turned into an office.

The male occupational health nurse asked him all the usual questions, and David just smiled, nodded, and reported that he felt fine and could carry out his duties without issue. The nurse ticked off a few boxes on the form clipped to his clipboard and told David he'd see him again in another three months. The whole appointment took less than five minutes.

At least it got me out of the office for a bit, David thought as he made his way back to the lifts and pressed the button.

As usual, the lift took its time, so while he waited, David pulled out his phone from his combat trousers pocket to text Jenn, letting her know how the appointment had gone.

Looking at the screen, a notification from his news feed caught his eye: *'Breaking News: Saudi Arabian king dies after long battle with cancer, son to take over.'*

David swiped the notification away and started texting Jenn as the lift doors finally opened. He stepped in and pressed the ground-floor button.

"Second floor… please… mind the doors…" the robotic voice echoed.

"We're on the sixth floor," David muttered in frustration as he glanced at his phone again.

The lift began its rattly descent, the lights flickering intermittently. David could hear the buzzing sound of electricity humming behind him.

Suddenly, the lift jerked to a stop and the lights went out.

"Shit," David muttered, fumbling to activate the torch on his phone. Lighting up the buttons on the lift wall, he started frantically pressing the one for the ground floor.

The robotic voice crackled back to life. "Sixth floor… Please wait…"

The lift jerked back to life, the lights flickering back on. David let out a huff of frustration.

Eventually, the lift stopped and the doors opened. When David stepped out, however, he realised something was off – this wasn't his floor.

By the looks of it, he'd ended up in the basement. It was dark, the air heavy with the scent of damp and mildew. Electrical cables hung from the ceiling, and there were pallets stacked with boxes – cleaning products and office supplies.

David felt a chill run down his spine; this place was very creepy indeed. He stepped back into the lift and frantically pressed the button for the ground floor, but nothing happened.

Then he heard whispers coming from behind him. The sound made the hairs on the back of his neck stand on end.

He quickly spun around, but the space behind him was empty – and yet, the whispers continued.

And they were growing louder.

Slowly, David stepped back out of the lift.

"Hello? Is there anyone there?" he called out, his voice echoing in the silence.

All he could hear now was his heartbeat pounding in his ears. He squinted into the darkness, feeling incredibly uneasy in the dark, dank basement.

David was edging further into the shadows when he

felt the unmistakable sensation of someone breathing on the back of his neck.

"David!"

He jumped, spinning around in a panic, but again, no one was there.

"Jesus Christ!" he exclaimed, breathless, as shock flooded through him.

As fast as he could, he turned around and ran back into the lift, pressing the ground-floor button again and again. His heart was pounding so fast he could barely catch his breath. He could hear the whispering behind him again.

He spun around once more, but again, there was no one there.

Panic surged through him as he leapt towards the button panel, slamming his finger on every button in sight until the doors finally closed. The moment they did, the whispering stopped.

Fear coursed through David's veins, tightening around his chest, and he was just beginning to hyperventilate when the doors opened again. Thankfully, this time, he was on the right floor.

He hurried out of the lift and exited the building, practically stumbling towards his car.

He had no idea what had just happened, but one thing was certain – he was completely and utterly freaked out.

***

David had hired a contracting company, Handymen Ltd, to finish building the staircase from the box room to the attic along with the door frame at the top of the stairs and of course the door itself. He had found them online and, due to their good reviews, he thought they were a safe bet. Though a bit of a ragtag team, they were experienced tradesmen who offered great banter – and, most importantly, the best and most reasonable quote. David was more than happy with the work they completed.

This gave David extra tasks like painting the door, spindles and door frame, although this didn't bother him in the slightest as he was happy that they were putting their own stamp on the house.

One Saturday afternoon, while Jenn was busy reorganising and decluttering the kids' bedroom and David was painting his and Jenn's bedroom, the two girls grew bored of painting pictures downstairs at the kitchen table. Quietly, they crept upstairs and into the attic, unseen by either of their parents.

When the staircase had been completed, David and Jenn warned the girls not to go up into the attic. It was dangerous, they told them, as there were lots of tools lying around and things that could hurt them. However, like curious cats, the kids ignored the warning and went up to explore the unfinished space.

The attic was like a building site. Half-finished wooden studwork loomed on the left side of the room. Long pieces of wood were piled up in a corner, and bags of plaster rested against the bare brick wall. Power tools, saws, and hand tools were strewn about haphazardly. Sawdust and wood shavings covered the floor, blending with layers of thick dust that had settled over many years.

In the far corner, an old dust sheet covered some old, forgotten furniture.

The only natural light came from a medium sized, filthy skylight on the right side of the slanted ceiling that overlooked the front garden; a shard of bright sunlight pierced through, illuminating the dust particles dancing in the air.

David and Jenn planned to install a modern Velux window, but like many DIY projects, progress had been slow, and completing the room would require both time and money.

Not understanding any of this, the girls crept into the room, carefully stepping around the scattered tools and materials, and navigating the attic floor as if they were in a minefield.

"This is going to be my room, Olivia," Bella whispered.

"Mine too!" Olivia cried out.

"Shh… we need to be quiet, remember?" Bella told her sister. "Mummy and Daddy said we're not allowed up here."

Olivia quickly put her hand over her mouth. "OK, Bella… I'll be quiet now," she whispered back.

Bella carefully moved around the room, gently touching the unfinished studwork. Olivia wandered over to the old furniture covered by the dust sheet, peeking under it. Something caught her eye under one of the chairs, though it was so dark under there she couldn't quite make out what it was. Bending down, she got on all fours and crawled under the chair. "Look, Bella… come and see what I've found!" she called out softly.

Bella turned around and crept towards her sister. "What is it, Olivia?"

Olivia had managed to pull the object out from under the chair, and as she crawled backwards and stood up, she held it out to show her sister. "I found a pencil, Bella... look!"

Bella squinted in the dim light, trying to figure out what it was. After a moment, her eyes widened in horror, and she let out a blood-curdling scream. "Ahhhh!" she yelled. "It's a finger!"

It was indeed a finger – a long, skinny, mummified one. The skin was discoloured, the fingernail long, ragged, and filthy. It was a truly horrifying find.

Startled by her sister's scream, Olivia also started screaming at the same time as she dropped the finger.

Downstairs in the main house, David and Jenn immediately froze. Then, dropping what they were doing, they rushed towards the sounds of the screaming, almost colliding with each other on the landing.

"Girls! Girls! Olivia? Bella? What's happened? Where are you?" Jenn shouted over the shrill screaming.

"They're in the attic!" David cried, panic creeping into his voice.

They both raced up to the attic room, their hearts pounding with fear, dreading the worst – that one of the girls had been hurt by the numerous hazardous tools and materials that were lying around up there.

David reached Bella first and scooped her up, while Jenn did the same with Olivia, both of them frantically checking for injuries.

"Calm down, Bella. What happened? Are you OK?

Did you hurt yourself?" David asked, his voice tight with concern.

"Finger… Olivia found a finger…" she replied, her voice shaky.

David blinked in confusion. "Olivia hurt her finger?" he asked, looking over at her.

"No," Bella said, her voice trembling. "Olivia *found* a finger." She then pointed to the floor where Olivia had dropped it.

David exchanged a worried glance with Jenn, who was holding Olivia tightly, trying to get her to stop crying. Jenn looked just as distressed as her daughter.

Pulling his phone out of his paint-covered tracksuit bottoms, David turned on the torch and scanned the floor where Bella was pointing. After a few moments, he spotted the finger – it was lying fingernail down. Moving closer for a better look, David could make out every detail of the severed appendage. It had been sheared off from the knuckle, and the nail seemed to have continued growing after it was severed, with dirt embedded beneath it.

"Oh my God!" Jenn gasped. "Where did that come from? And how long has it been there? Do you think we should call the police?"

"I don't know, Jenn," David replied, shaking his head, "it looks like it's been here for a while… it was probably a work accident or something, many years ago. I doubt the police would be interested."

"That's horrific," Jenn replied, pulling her gaze away from the finger. "Well, come on, girls – let's go downstairs and wash your hands. And what did Mummy and Daddy tell you both about being up here? It's dangerous

– you could have been hurt!" She shook her head angrily. "David, can you get rid of it, please?"

"Yeah," David replied. "I'll wrap it up and put it in the bin outside. I'll be down in a minute."

Jenn led the girls – who had just about stopped crying – downstairs, while David stood up and looked around the floor. He spotted an old, dirty rag, picked it up, and shook it to rid it of excess sawdust. He then bent down, carefully picked up the finger with the rag, and wrapped it tightly.

After a moment, he went downstairs and placed it in the outside wheelie bin, a cold shiver shooting down his spine as he closed the lid. He then hurried back inside to wash his hands and check on the kids.

Jenn had managed to calm them down, but they were both still shaken up.

So was David.

***

It was Sunday evening, and Jenn had put the two kids in the bath while she put some washing away and prepared their school and nursery clothes for the week ahead. When she'd finished her task, she got the kids out of the bath, wrapped them in towels, and brought them into her and David's bedroom.

As she was drying them off, she noticed various small bruises on the backs of their legs, shoulders, and upper arms.

"Girls... where did these bruises come from?" she asked, concern creeping into her voice.

Bella and Olivia both shrugged.

"I don't know, Mummy," Bella said quietly.

Jenn frowned. "Well, you must know where they came from. They look like finger marks."

"I think I got them from nursery, Mummy," Olivia said after a moment.

Jenn's concern deepened. "Is someone hurting you at nursery, Olivia?"

"No, Mummy. I love my friends at nursery. They don't hurt me at all," Olivia replied, shaking her head.

Jenn turned to Bella. "What about you, Bella? Is anyone hurting you at school?"

Bella shook her head. "No, Mummy. I would tell you and Daddy if anyone was hitting me."

Jenn smiled, relieved, though still worried. She believed them both, but then what were these marks? "Good girls," she told them. "Now, come on, let's get your pyjamas on."

Once they were both dressed, Jenn called out to David, who was downstairs making packed lunches for the next day. "David? Can you come up here for a minute?"

David stopped what he was doing and marched up the stairs, heading into the bedroom where Jenn and the kids were. "What's up, sweetheart?" he asked as he walked into the room.

"Come and have a look at these bruises that have suddenly appeared on the kids," Jenn replied, her concern evident.

David knelt down on the carpet to inspect the bruises, tutting softly. "They're probably just bruises from playing kids' games," he said, trying to reassure her. "I'm sure it's nothing to worry about."

Jenn frowned. "But they look like finger marks, David. Look again."

David sighed. "Yes, I can see that, Jenn, but kids get bruises. It's just part of growing up."

Jenn sighed deeply, clearly frustrated.

David shrugged. "OK, look, I'll show you." He turned to the kids. "Right, you two, lie down on the carpet for a moment, please."

The kids giggled as David grabbed them both by the ankles and dragged them towards him, at which point he started tickling them all over.

Jenn sighed and rolled her eyes. "But that doesn't prove anything!" she protested.

David didn't hear what Jenn had said over the loud giggling of the kids. So, she tapped his shoulder and he turned to face her.

"What, sweetheart?"

"I said that doesn't prove anything."

"OK, kids… freeze!" David commanded.

The kids immediately stopped giggling and froze, as still as statues. David lifted Bella's leg and pulled up her pyjamas to expose the back of her legs. Sure enough, there were fresh red finger marks that matched David's hands. He then did the same with Olivia's leg, revealing identical red marks.

"See?" he said to Jenn. "I just gave the kids finger marks by playing with them for a couple of seconds. Now, just think what they get up to in school and at nursery."

David went back to tickling and playing with the kids, while Jenn rolled her eyes and sighed again.

"You've always got to be right, don't you, David?"

David looked up and smiled. "Yup, pretty much. Look, you've got to stop being so negative and thinking everything has a sinister undertone to it."

"Well, in my line of work, it usually does," Jenn replied.

By now, the kids were giggling even louder and bouncing around with excitement.

"David! Please don't get them all riled up; I'm just about to put them to bed," Jenn cried, shaking her head. "Oh, David… you always do this! I try to put them to bed, and you get them all hyper!"

"Right, OK kids, you heard Mummy – it's bedtime," David told them. "Daddy needs to go and finish making up the lunches. Goodnight, my beautiful girls."

He gave the kids a quick kiss and made his escape, just as the carnage of a hyperactive bedtime was about to unfold.

Jenn closed her eyes, rubbed her face, and sighed heavily.

***

It was 3.42 am, and everyone in the house was sleeping soundly when, all of a sudden, an almighty thud jolted David and Jenn awake. David quickly sat up and cocked his head, trying to pinpoint the source of the noise.

"What was tha-"

David held up a hand, interrupting his wife. "Shh…"

Thud… thud… thud

"It's coming from the kitchen," David whispered,

jumping out of bed and rushing to the wardrobe to retrieve his trusty baseball bat. "Stay here, and don't move. I'll check on the kids."

Jenn nodded, concern written all over her face.

David crept out of the bedroom, slowly approached the girls' room, and opened the door just a crack. They were both sleeping peacefully. So, he gently closed the door, eased open the baby gate, and began to descend the stairs. He rested the bat over his right shoulder, his grip firm on the handle. His heart was pounding, adrenaline coursing through his veins. As he approached the closed kitchen door, he forced himself to steady his breath.

He paused, listening for any more noises. There were none – just deafening silence, broken only by the rhythmic thumping of his heart, galloping in his chest like a wild stallion.

Taking a deep breath, David mentally counted to three before bursting through the door, left shoulder first, the baseball bat raised above his head, ready to strike.

But there was no one there.

He flicked on the kitchen light and slowly scanned every inch of the kitchen. Nothing was amiss. Nothing was out of place. There were no signs whatsoever of any kind of intruder.

Slowly, David walked into the dining area, continuing to scan everything at lightning speed, like some kind of Terminator searching for a threat to immobilise. He found nothing.

He went over to the door and checked it was locked. It was. He checked every window, then crept into the front living room and scanned the space. Everything was where it should be – nothing out of place or missing. He checked the windows. All secure.

David came out of the living room and closed the door. He checked the front door – that was locked too.

Looking around one more time, he lifted the baseball bat off his shoulder and slowly brought it to his side. Then, he quietly crept back upstairs.

"David?... David? Is that you?" Jenn whispered.

"Yeah, it's me," David replied, entering the bedroom and placing the bat above the wardrobe where it belonged.

"Well?" Jenn pressed, when he didn't say anything. "What was it? What made that loud bang?"

"Nothing," David said bluntly.

Jenn frowned. "What do you mean, nothing? We both heard something, right? It was so loud it woke us up!"

David rubbed his face. "Yes, I'm aware of that, Jenn, but I've just checked everywhere and nothing is out of place, nothing has been moved, and all the windows and doors are locked."

"Well, what made that noise then?" Jenn asked. "And are the girls OK?"

David sighed. "Yes, they're fine, sound asleep. And I don't know what made the noise, Jenn, but there's definitely no intruder in the house."

Jenn was still frowning. "I don't know, David, that was a pretty loud bang... something must have caused it..."

David got back into bed and threw the duvet over himself. "Well... if you want to go down and check, you're more than welcome. But I'm going back to sleep," he said with a yawn.

Jenn felt uneasy and, unfortunately, couldn't get back to sleep. She stayed awake all night, straining to listen for any more unsettling noises in the house.

***

Olivia had been sent home from nursery with a vomiting and diarrhoea bug, and – since his caseload was lighter that month – David had asked his boss if he could work from home for a few days to look after his daughter.

Olivia had fallen asleep on David after they'd spent most of the morning watching cartoons. David was feeling tired, his eyes growing heavier, until a loud noise suddenly echoed from upstairs.

Thud... thud... thud...

David froze, suddenly alert.

After a moment, he heard it again, this time louder than before.

Thud... thud... thud...

David's stomach churned. He and Olivia were the only ones in the house, and all the doors and windows were locked. So where was this mysterious noise coming from?

Carefully, he lifted Olivia off him, gently laying her across the couch with her head resting on a cushion. He then draped her pink unicorn blanket over her to keep her warm.

With that done, David set off to investigate.

He slowly climbed the stairs, the thudding growing ever louder and more aggressive.

Thud... thud... thud... thud...

It was coming from the loft.

His heart pounding and his body tense, David slowly walked up the attic stairs.

Upon entering the attic, he slowly looked around.

Thud... thud... thud...

The banging startled him, and he turned, trying to locate the source.

Slowly, he edged towards the eaves cupboard door, squinting in the dim light.

Thud... thud... thud...

David saw the eaves door open and close, so he dropped to his knees and opened the door, feeling a cold draught blow against his face. He leaned in, peering through the cupboard and looking around.

He let out a sigh of relief as his body relaxed. *Mystery solved,* he thought.

There was a small hole in the corner of the eaves, and that's where the drought was getting in, causing the cupboard door to make the loud thudding noise. It would be an easy fix – just a bit of expanding foam to fill the hole and then some tightening of the cupboard door hinges.

Satisfied, David closed the cupboard door and grabbed his electric jigsaw box, placing it against the door to hold it shut. He then stood, surveying the rest of the attic room. As he mentally assessed the jobs that needed to be done to make the space habitable, he took notes of how long it would take him, how much it would cost, and – more importantly – when he'd be able to find the time to complete it.

He was just letting out a disheartened sigh when, suddenly, another loud thud echoed through the house, followed by Olivia's cry. David's whole body tensed up again, and he raced downstairs to find Olivia lying on the living room floor, crying. She had fallen off the couch while she was sleeping.

David scooped her up and gave her a cuddle to comfort her. It took about five minutes to settle her, after which she fell back to sleep in his arms.

***

Jenn was jolted awake by the sound of thudding somewhere in the house. She looked at David, who was lying on his side, snoring loudly. She checked the time on her phone – it was 2:41 am.

Picking up the baby monitor, she activated the LCD display and a message appeared on the screen: *'No signal detected.'* One of the kids must have unplugged the camera, she thought.

Jenn cocked her head, trying to pinpoint the source of the noise. Then, another loud thump echoed from the kids' room.

As panic surged through her, Jenn threw the duvet off and jumped out of bed, hurrying to the girls' bedroom. She opened the baby gate across the doorway and stepped into the room.

Peering into the dimly lit space, Jenn tried to make out the shapes of the kids in their beds, and as her eyes adjusted to the low light, she realised Bella wasn't in hers. Her little duvet was crumpled in the middle of the mattress, and Bella was nowhere to be seen.

Once again, panic shot through Jenn's body as another thud sounded from the far corner of the room. Her heart raced.

She quickly reached for the landing light switch just outside the kids' room and flicked it on.

Light flooded into the room, revealing Bella standing in front of the bookcase in the corner, as if she were trying to walk through it. Her head was tilted to one side.

Jenn took a few cautious steps forward, softly calling out, "Bella? Bella, are you OK?"

As she got closer, Bella turned around, her eyes were half shut, raised her left arm, and pointed at Jenn. Before Jenn could even respond, Bella began screaming hysterically.

The sound of Bella's scream woke Olivia, who immediately started crying. Jenn dropped to her knees, trying to comfort her, but it was no use – it only made things worse. Now, both girls were screaming at the top of their lungs.

David, still half asleep, jumped out of bed in a blind panic and rushed towards the source of the screams. "What the hell is going on?" he shouted over the noise, before scooping up Olivia and holding her tight in an attempt to calm her.

"Bella was sleepwalking, and now she's having a nightmare!" Jenn shouted back. "I think…"

David quickly handed Olivia to Jenn, who went back into their bedroom, trying to soothe her. Meanwhile, David turned his attention to Bella, attempting to calm her down as well. After a few moments, she stopped screaming. She opened her eyes, and when she saw

David, she threw her arms around his neck and began to sob.

"It's OK, sweetheart, it was just a bad dream. Mummy and Daddy are here now," David reassured her, gently stroking her hair.

"Daddy, I saw a man standing there with a werewolf mask on. He was really scary!" Bella wailed.

"But darling, it wasn't real. It was just a bad dream," he told her, before picking her up in his arms and walking through to his and Jenn's bedroom. Jenn was sitting on the bed, gently rocking Olivia backwards and forwards. Olivia had now calmed down, though she was still crying.

David sat down next to Jenn. "She said she had a dream about a man wearing a werewolf mask standing in her room," he told her.

Jenn gave him a concerned look, her brow furrowing as she glanced at Bella. "Sweetheart, it's OK," she said softly. "Mummy came in to check on you and your sister because I heard you sleepwalking. When I came in, you were standing by your bookcase, and then you turned around."

"I know, and then I saw the scary man!" Bella wailed, burying her face into her dad's shoulder.

David gently rubbed her back, trying to soothe her, while whispering reassurances that everything was OK. When he looked over at his wife, he could tell what she was thinking.

Everything was most definitely *not* OK.

Chapter 11

At 3:07 am, David – who'd been sleeping deeply on his back – woke up to the sound of what he thought were the kids playing downstairs. He groaned loudly, not wanting to get out of bed to sort them out.

Then, as his eyes fluttered open, he froze. In the doorway of the bedroom stood a tall, dark figure, staring directly at him. A wave of fear and terror swept over David as the hair on the back of his neck stood up.

The figure was almost entirely a shadow, but what held David's attention were the figure's eyes – they were burning into him, glowing in an unnatural way. The whites of the eye were actually yellow, the iris was blood red, and the pupils – black and vertical – resembled those of a cat or a snake.

David could still hear the kids downstairs; it sounded like they were jumping on and off the furniture and generally running amok, playing and giggling, as they usually did during the day. Beyond the figure, he could see flashing images, as if the kids' TV was on in their room, though there was no sound. These flashing images – combined with the house's utter darkness – bathed the mysterious figure in an eerie dim light, making it look even more unsettling.

In this moment, David's main concern was getting to the kids and checking they were OK, but his body was completely paralysed. Whether this was from fear or the presence of this supernatural figure in the doorway, he couldn't tell. What he did know was that his heart rate was increasing and that he'd broken out into a cold sweat. His eyes darted around the room, desperately trying to escape this nightmare.

Jenn was lying peacefully on her side, just inches from David's right shoulder, completely unaware of the terror unfolding around them. He tried to call out to her, but his mouth wouldn't cooperate. He couldn't speak – not even a whisper or a mumble.

He wriggled, trying to move – anything to wake her up – but he was utterly helpless. Jenn rolled over onto her other side, her back now to him, oblivious to the horror in the room.

David's eyes snapped back to the figure still standing in the doorway, staring him down. It took a deep breath, then let out a low, guttural growl – like a dog or a wolf. David's heart raced even faster – it felt as though it might burst from his chest.

Suddenly, David felt a strange tingling sensation spreading throughout his entire body, and as he glanced up, he saw that the ceiling was slowly coming towards him. Panic surged through him as he looked back at the carpeted floor and saw it getting farther and farther away.

Horrified, he locked eyes on the figure standing in the doorway at the same time as he realised something utterly unbelievable – he was levitating off the bed. The duvet slipped off him as he rose, still paralysed, his body stiff as a board.

He paused briefly in mid-air, sweat pouring from his brow – it dripped down his face and the back of his neck, soaking into the carpet below. Then, ever so slowly, he started moving towards the figure.

David had never been so terrified in his whole life.

His heart hammering against his chest, he squeezed his eyes shut, trying to steady his breathing. He'd almost got it under control when the strange sensation in his body disappeared. He snapped his eyes open, seeing the ceiling rapidly moving away from him again. He was falling.

With a sudden, jarring thud, he landed on the carpet, the impact so intense he thought it would wake the entire house – and probably the neighbours too. Unfortunately, it didn't; Jenn was still sleeping peacefully in the bed.

Dazed and confused, David struggled to get his bearings. He was lying on his back in a crumpled heap, the figure still standing over him. Its eyes – those terrifying, evil eyes – were still locked on him, and it was breathing heavily. This time, the figure let out a louder growl.

From David's point of view, the figure seemed upside down, as he was lying at its feet, staring up in sheer terror, still paralysed.

The figure bent over then, moving closer to his face until it was just inches away, still growling and breathing heavily. David started to hyperventilate.

The rancid stench of rotten meat hit David like a physical blow. The smell was unbearable, so much so that he choked and gagged.

The figure smiled, pursed its lips, and then – in a thick German accent – it spoke: "I… will… take… all… of… your… SOULS!"

It screamed, and just when David thought he couldn't take it anymore, his body jerked violently and he woke with a start, finding himself on the floor in the bedroom doorway. Daylight streamed through the curtains. It was morning.

Sweating, confused, and panting – with his heart still racing – David took a moment to orient himself. At least he had full control of his body again. So, without hesitation, he jumped up and rushed to the kids' bedroom. They were both still in their beds, sleeping soundly, just as he had left them the night before.

David let out a silent sigh of relief. His heart rate began to slow as the fear gradually melted away, but the memory of the nightmare still lingered.

He checked the kids' TV first – it was switched off at the wall. He then went downstairs to ensure every door and window was securely closed and locked. Everything was as it should be. Next, he checked both TVs in the living rooms – front and back – just to see if they'd been left on overnight. He wondered if leaving one of the TVs on might have somehow influenced the nightmare he'd experienced. Sure enough, both were switched off at the plugs.

Obviously, it had just been a nightmare, he told

himself – a truly terrifying, vivid nightmare that had seemed completely and utterly real.

David went into the kitchen, made himself a coffee from the machine, and sat at the dining table. The events of the previous night had left him incredibly shaken, and he couldn't stop replaying the nightmare in his mind. *Was it a nightmare, or was it real?* he pondered. *And how did I end up on the floor?* Maybe he'd been sleepwalking.

Curious, David googled what he'd experienced, and from what he could see, it sounded very much like sleep paralysis. He'd heard of this before.

'Sleep paralysis can occur,' he read, '*when the brain is in a dreamlike state while the body believes it's still asleep. The dreamer can experience hallucinations of intruders or other terrifying visions. It typically happens during transitions between wakefulness and sleep, when the person may be unable to move or speak for a few seconds or even minutes. Some people also feel pressure on their chest or a sensation of choking. It often occurs when one has irregular sleep patterns or hasn't been getting enough sleep.*'

That makes sense, David thought. Sleep was not something he was getting a lot of these days.

He tried to push the unsettling thoughts to the back of his mind and enjoy the peace and quiet while he drank his coffee. Looking at the kitchen clock, he saw it was 6:12 am. The kids would be getting up soon.

Still, David couldn't shake the haunting feeling he'd got from the nightmare. It lingered throughout the day, affecting his concentration at work.

On the drive home, he noticed an ironmongers and hardware shop on the corner of the high street, and he remembered what Matt had told him about the iron shavings. *What do I have to lose?* he thought, pulling over and heading into the shop.

David had a quick look around before going up to the counter.

An elderly Scotsman, wearing a long brown work overcoat, greeted him with a warm smile. "Good afternoon, my friend. What can I do for you?"

David smiled and cleared his throat. "Hello there. This is going to sound strange, but I was wondering if you had any spare iron shavings you could sell me?"

The man's smile faded, and a look of confusion crossed his face. "Iron shavings? What do you want with iron shavings, son?"

David scrambled to come up with an explanation. After a moment, he managed to reply, "Umm… my daughter's working on a science project at school… something to do with magnets and iron shavings…" He shrugged, laughing. "I don't really know."

The man's face broke into a smile. "Ah, I see… she's a clever little cookie then, eh? Alright, let's see what we've got under here…" He bent over and rummaged around under the counter until he found what he was looking for. "Ah ha, here it is!" he exclaimed, pulling a box from beneath the counter and placing it in front of David.

Inside the box were several long, thin spirals of metal of various sizes.

"Now, what you want to do," the man continued, "is when you get home, put on a pair of gardening gloves and break it up into wee bits. Don't do it with your bare hands, or you'll tear your skin to ribbons."

David smiled. "Thank you kindly. How much do I owe you?"

The man held up a hand and smiled back. "No charge, son. It was all just going to go in the bin anyway. I'm glad it's getting put to better use."

"Thank you very much," said David, taking the box, "I appreciate it."

"Cheerio, son."

David stepped out of the shop, feeling a small sense of accomplishment. *That's one job done,* he thought. *Now I just need to get some holy water.*

***

It was a Thursday afternoon, and David was sitting in his office, finishing up some patient notes on his laptop. When he finished, he glanced at his watch: 2:26 pm. *Coffee time*, he thought.

He headed to the kitchen area, made himself a cup of coffee, and returned to his desk. As he sipped his drink, his mind wandered to the strange events that had been happening at home recently, so he decided to google the history of his house – what year it was built, how many previous owners or occupants it had, that kind of thing.

He soon found copies of the land registry details for the property, and as he read them, something odd stood out to him. Nearly all of the occupants had only lived in the house for around 18 months to two years – bar one, who had lived in the property for about 25 years, from 1946 until 1970. After that, the house remained vacant for a number of years, and then the same pattern repeated itself.

After taking this in, David searched for statistics on how long the average family stays in a house. The results varied, with some sources saying between eight and 13.5 years, while most suggested 21 to 35 years. This made sense to David – families usually move when their children get older and fly the nest, and parents typically downsize as they reach retirement.

So why is this house different? he wondered.

He then started researching the history of the area, searching for information like census returns, when the area was urbanised, what was there before, and property price history. What he found seemed unremarkable at first – the area had been mostly farmland until the turn of the century, when the local council started buying up all the land to build new houses. Then, World War I broke out, and construction was put on hold.

Work on David's house began in 1933 and was completed in 1936, along with most of the other houses on the estate. World War II disrupted the building process once more in 1939, halting construction to support the war effort.

Pretty standard stuff, David thought.

He continued digging through census returns and came across a list of past occupants. That's when he stumbled upon an old, recently digitised local newspaper article about a holocaust survivor named Benjamin Goldman, who had come to settle in the UK after the war.

David studied the old, grainy, black-and-white picture on his laptop screen, his gaze fixed on the figure staring back at him. He recognised the name from the census returns, and a strange, unsettling feeling began to stir in his stomach – one he couldn't quite explain.

As he continued to study the image, the battery icon on his laptop flashed an empty battery graphic before quickly disappearing – David had forgotten to put the laptop on charge, and the screen had now gone black.

Just as he glanced away from it, out of the corner of his eye, he caught a glimpse of something that made his heart stop. The grotesque face from his nightmare was staring back at him just over his left shoulder, in the reflection of the laptop screen.

David jumped back in shock, his pulse racing. He tried to turn around, but in his panic, he lost his balance and fell off his computer chair, landing hard on the office's carpeted floor.

Shaken and disoriented, David quickly looked around the room, but there was nothing there. He glanced at his watch – 4.45 pm.

"Shit!" he muttered to himself. "I'm going to be late picking up the kids!"

He scrambled to his feet, gathered up all his belongings, and shoved them in his backpack before running out of the office and jumping in his car.

The drive to collect the kids was a blur. His mind kept replaying the moment his laptop ran out of charge, and the horrifying face he'd seen over his shoulder. It had given him the creeps. The more he thought about it, the more his mind started to race – and the more he questioned himself. Were his eyes just playing tricks on him? Was he too stressed with the house, work, and the kids?

Or were he and his family really being haunted by some strange paranormal entity?

David stopped at a set of traffic lights, watching the world go by for a moment, lost in thought. *Maybe we need a break*, he mused. *A short caravan holiday or a cheap week away to Spain... anywhere to break up the mundane routine.*

He glanced in his rearview mirror and froze.

There, sitting in the back seat, was the same grotesque face he'd just seen in the reflection of his blank laptop screen. The figure had sharp, ragged features, its skin coated in what appeared to be coal dust or dirt. It wore torn, filthy clothes, and its eyes – yellow and red, just like the shadowy figure from his nightmare a few weeks ago – stared back at him.

Before he could react, the creature opened its mouth and let out a blood-curdling scream, making David jump.

By the time he turned around to check the back seat, there was nothing there – the figure had gone.

His breath came in quick, shallow gasps, and his chest tightened with panic.

A long, angry car horn blared behind him, snapping him back to reality. The traffic lights had turned green.

Quickly, David checked his rearview mirror before putting the car into gear and driving off. *I definitely need a holiday*, he thought, as he decided to keep this experience – and all recent experiences – to himself. He didn't need the inevitable 'I told you so' speech from Jenn right now.

When he got home, he suggested to Jenn that they

take the kids away for the long weekend. Jenn's parents had a caravan down by the coast, less than an hour's drive from the city, which they used as a holiday home. Jenn loved the idea, especially since she'd been struggling to come up with plans for the upcoming bank holiday weekend.

So, it was decided and planned, and the kids were already getting excited; they always enjoyed their trips to the caravan.

***

It was the Friday afternoon of the bank holiday weekend and David had just finished with his last patient. The plan was simple – pick up the kids from school and nursery, grab Jenn from work, and then hit the road before rush hour traffic started. David had packed the car the night before, eager to avoid wasting time during the afternoon rush.

Once he'd picked up Jenn and the kids, they were on their way.

However, by the time they hit the motorway, it seemed like everyone else had the same idea – especially as the weather forecast promised sunny days all weekend.

They got stuck in light traffic for around 15 minutes when they first got on the motorway, but David didn't care. He desperately needed this break, so he wasn't going to let anything spoil it. The traffic soon cleared anyway, and they were on their way again.

Around 45 minutes later, they reached the sleepy coastal town and stopped at a local supermarket for 'supplies' as Jenn called them. This shopping included booze for herself and David, sweets and snacks for the kids, and a few pizzas for dinner. They also got some picnic stuff for the beach the next day.

That evening, after Jenn had made up the picnic food and put it all in the fridge, David put the kids to bed. They fell asleep quickly, exhausted from the excitement – with the fresh sea air probably helping too.

Next, David headed to the kitchen, where Jenn was tidying up and cleaning the surfaces. He poured her a gin and tonic and grabbed a bottle of beer for himself. They smiled at each other and clinked their drinks together.

"Cheers!" they said in unison.

"Do you fancy sitting out on the decking with these?" Jenn asked, after taking a sip.

"You read my mind – let's go," David replied with a smile.

It was a beautiful, warm spring evening, and the sky was clear, with not a cloud in sight. They were surrounded by lush, green, rolling hills, and in the distance, there were lambs, horses, and cows grazing in the fields.

David collapsed into a deckchair, put his sunglasses on, took a long sip of his beer, and let out a satisfied sigh. "This is bliss, isn't it, Jenn? We definitely needed this break."

"Yeah, it's lovely here," Jenn agreed. "And yes, this was one of your better ideas."

David turned to Jenn and smiled.

They stayed out on the deck, having a few drinks until the sun went down, then they went back inside and headed to bed.

The next morning, the kids were up early, as usual,

excited to go to the beach. David and Jenn had two very strong coffees each, gave the kids their breakfast, and then got themselves washed and dressed. Finally, Jenn got the kids ready while David loaded the car, and they all headed to the beach.

They arrived at around 9:45 am, when the beach was pretty much empty – just a few dog walkers and joggers. They found a nice spot and laid out the blanket. The tide was out, and there was a bit of a breeze. A low mist stretched across the beach, but the sun was shining, and it was still warm.

After a while, Jenn took the kids down to the shoreline to paddle and hunt for shells, while David kicked off his trainers, removed his socks, and stretched out on the picnic blanket. It was the most relaxed he'd felt in a long time. So much so that he fell asleep in the warm sunshine.

With everything that had been going on at the house recently, along with the daily stresses of work and family life, David had forgotten to appreciate the important things. Breaking up the routine was exactly what he'd needed.

He was awoken suddenly by a shower of sandy seashells and drips of cold seawater as the kids dumped what seemed like hundreds of shells on top of him.

"Daddy… Daddy! Look at all the shells we found!" Bella shouted. "Mummy said we can paint them when we get home!"

"Oh, wow, that is a lot of shells, isn't it? They'll all look lovely painted," David replied, admiring the collection. He looked at his watch – it was 11:14 am. The sun had gotten warmer, the low mist had cleared, and there were now a lot more people on the beach. With the warm sun on his skin and a cool, fresh breeze floating in from the sea, David thought he could have been in the Mediterranean.

Jenn arrived at the picnic blanket shortly after the kids. "You should go down and have a paddle, David," she suggested. "The water is lovely."

David looked up at her, raising an eyebrow. "Is it? It looks cold to me," he said with a grin. "I might go for a paddle after lunch." He turned to the girls. "Right, kids, come and get a sandwich!"

They all huddled together and ate their sandwiches and snacks while enjoying the sunshine.

"Daddy," Bella said after a while, "I don't want my crusts. You can have them if you like," she added, handing them to him.

"Me too," said Olivia, doing the same.

"I can't eat all these crusts! Are you two trying to get Daddy fat?" David asked in a funny voice, making the girls giggle. "We'll give them to the seagulls. After all, it's their lunchtime too," he added with a wink. He threw the crusts onto the sand, about four metres or so from the blanket, and the seagulls immediately started squawking and diving towards the food. Soon enough, there were about six or seven gulls all fighting over the crusts.

"Silly birdies!" Olivia giggled.

Once the crusts were gone, the seagulls took flight in search of more food. A moment later, a jackdaw landed on the sand, pecking around for any crumbs the gulls had overlooked.

"Aww, look, Daddy... that bird didn't get any bread!" Bella exclaimed.

"Poor little birdy," said Olivia, who was in the middle of eating a packet of crisps. She then stood up, walked over to the bird, and emptied the crisp packet onto the sand, before running quickly back to the blanket.

The bird eyed the crisps, pecked at them, and then looked up, staring back at the family.

The seagulls returned almost immediately, and again proceeded to scavenge and fight over the crisps, squawking loudly. The jackdaw, however, remained still, watching the four of them intently.

"Silly birdy, you didn't get any crisps!" Bella cried.

Jenn frowned. "What's it doing, David?"

"I don't know," he replied, "just staring at us for some reason..."

In truth, he was starting to feel uneasy. He kept his eyes fixed on the little bird, which was now staring directly at him. Feeling uncomfortable, David picked up a driftwood stick, snapped it in two, and threw it at the bird. "Go on... get out of here, you creepy little bird!" he muttered.

The girls started giggling.

"Yeah, go away, silly bird!" Bella shouted.

The twig landed a few feet from the bird, but it didn't move an inch.

Annoyed, David picked up a pebble and threw it at the bird. This time, the pebble landed mere inches away from it, but again, the bird didn't even flinch. It just continued to stare at David with its eerie, piercing green eyes.

Jenn laughed, and the kids quickly followed suit. "That little bird is mugging you off, David!"

"Yeah, it looks like it, the cheeky little sod," he replied, before standing up and running towards the bird. "Go on, get out of here!" he yelled.

The bird still didn't move – until he was about a foot away from it, at which point it flew off.

"He wasn't so brave then, was he, girls?" David asked with a big grin.

Jenn and the kids burst out laughing.

"Silly Daddy!" Olivia shouted, still giggling.

David turned around and looked up to see where the bird had flown away to. It was nowhere in sight. However, the uneasy feeling that he was being watched lingered.

Jenn wanted a family picture of the four of them on the beach, so she asked a middle-aged couple walking their dog to take the photo. They happily obliged as Jenn handed the lady her phone and got into position.

The kids were sitting on the blanket, with David and Jenn kneeling behind them, their backs to the sea. The sun was beaming down on them all, giving them a healthy glow.

The lady snapped a few pictures and handed Jenn her phone back.

The kids made a fuss over the couple's dog, which wouldn't go near David and seemed very wary of him, growling every couple of minutes.

David found this strange, as dogs and most other animals always came to him, but he quickly dismissed the feeling. Ignoring the dog, he exchanged pleasantries with the old couple for a few moments before they left.

David, Jenn, and the kids stayed at the beach for most of the day, then returned to the caravan to shower and have dinner. They spent the rest of the bank holiday weekend at the local park and exploring the quaint little village shops.

It felt like a much-needed mini holiday, and soon, it was Monday afternoon and time to drive back home. The kids slept for most of the journey, and David and Jenn enjoyed the relaxing, comfortable silence as the beautiful scenery whizzed past them. Soon enough, they were back to the reality of the concrete jungle that was urban city life.

Chapter 12

On the Tuesday morning after the bank holiday weekend, David arrived at work early to find an empty office. He plugged his laptop into the mains and turned it on.

Once it had started up and he'd logged in, the main home page appeared. All the window tabs he'd been browsing before his laptop had died on Friday afternoon were still open. He began closing them one by one, but stopped when something caught his eye – something he'd clearly missed before.

There were three separate local newspaper articles about missing persons, all from different time periods: the 1970s, 1980s, and 1990s.

His blood ran cold as he recognised the face in one of the photos. It was the girl from the CCTV footage.

His mind racing, he read all about the girl – Katie McKinnon.

Katie was an ordinary 18-year-old girl. She had left

school at 15 and worked at the local supermarket. She lived with her mum, dad, and her little brother. Katie was a happy, outgoing person – until her mum died suddenly from a brain aneurysm. Afterwards, Katie spiralled into a deep depression.

Her mental health deteriorated further, and she began exhibiting paranoid schizophrenic behaviour. Eventually, she was committed to the local mental health hospital, where she underwent electroconvulsive therapy (ECT).

But somehow, Katie managed to escape from the hospital and was reported missing. She was last seen wearing only a hospital gown and no shoes. She was never found.

The article was dated the 3rd of May, 1971.

David stared at the screen for several minutes, trying to wrap his head around what he was seeing. 1971? How was that even possible?

His heart pounded in his chest as he moved on to the next article, which gave the details of the next missing person from their area.

James 'Jim' Maxwell was a middle-aged man who worked as a park keeper at the local park. He also had a part-time job as a night watchman at a nearby bus depot. He was happily married with three teenage children, and he was known to be a heavy smoker.

One time, when he was at home alone, a fire broke out in the house, and when the fire brigade arrived, his body was nowhere to be found. The fire department later released a statement saying that the fire was accidental, most likely caused by a discarded cigarette. Jim was last seen wearing his black night watchman uniform.

The article was dated the 6th of October, 1983.

David forced himself to read the next article.

Andrew 'Andy' Thomas was a happy, outgoing six-year-old boy. He loved going to school, had lots of friends, and enjoyed drawing, colouring, and playing. One summer, he went missing from his back garden and was never found. He had dark brown hair with a bowl cut, and was last seen wearing yellow *Power Rangers* shorts, a *Toy Story* T-shirt, and *Sonic the Hedgehog* trainers.

This article was dated the 10th of July, 1995.

"Oh my God!" David muttered, unable to believe what he was seeing.

These articles all had one thing in common – these people had all lived in the same house, just at different points in time.

A freezing cold shiver trickled down David's spine. What did all of this mean? What had happened to these people? And how exactly were these cases connected? He didn't know, but he was determined to find out.

He printed copies of all the articles and placed them in a folder in his laptop backpack. He knew he was going to need all the information he could get his hands on.

His mind continued to race with questions. Why had a missing girl from the 1970s been seen outside his house? Why was a missing child from the 1990s playing with his kids in his back garden? And why was there no record of the fire when he and Jenn had bought the house?

Determined to find answers, David called the solicitor who had handled the house sale.

After a lengthy and very boring conversation with the lawyer, it turned out that because the fire had occurred so many years ago, it wasn't required to be disclosed. That made sense, considering the home report David had received when he first expressed interest in the house. This report stated that the property had undergone a full rewire and renovation back in 1983 / 1984, with no updates since. This was likely why they'd managed to get it so cheap – it needed modernising, especially the electrics.

One mystery solved, David thought. But what about the other two?

***

Hanns Dietrich Fritz

1912 - 1970

Hanns Dietrich Fritz was a highly intelligent, well-educated young man, born in Munich on the 3rd of May, 1912. He hailed from a wealthy, aristocratic family. Handsome, with a chiselled chin, sharp features, short, dark hair, and a tall, slim athletic build, he cut an imposing figure.

However, despite his outward success, Hanns harboured a secret: he was a closeted homosexual.

Contrary to popular belief, homosexuality wasn't actually outlawed in Germany during this period; in fact, some might argue that Europe was ahead of its time regarding sexual revolutions in the 1930s and 1940s. However, Hanns's traditional and religious family would never have accepted such a lifestyle. As a result, he was forced to suppress these feelings, though occasionally, he would secretly visit underground gay clubs and speakeasies.

Hanns appreciated the finer things in life. He indulged in fine wines and dined at the best restaurants, often in the company of powerful individuals – he had friends in very high places. He had a deep love for classical music, with a particular fondness for Bach and Beethoven, and he was a frequent visitor to the opera.

He was also an evil, sadistic Nazi German SS officer during World War II, overseeing the day-to-day operations of many of the concentration camps. His cruelty was so extreme that it made figures like Ivan The Terrible seem saintly by comparison.

Thanks to his family's connections, he was given the comfortable post overseeing the running of the camps, rather than being sent to the front lines. He found particular enjoyment in the horrors of the camps, especially in supervising the brutal medical experiments and torturous practices carried out by doctors and scientists on the prisoners.

Like many of his contemporaries – such as Heinrich Himmler – Hanns was deeply obsessed with the occult, demonology, Devil worship, witchcraft, and anything paranormal or supernatural. His interest in these dark subjects began at a young age, and he studied them extensively throughout his life.

On occasion, he even conducted his own experiments with the prisoners, attempting to summon evil spirits, demons, and – at one point – the Devil himself, through human sacrifice. He also used his powerful Nazi connections to try and obtain the original first edition of the *Grimoire*, a spellbook from the 15th century written by satanic witches for consulting demons for personal gain. However, despite his obsession, his efforts to consult with demonic entities were never realised.

Hanns knew that Germany would not win the war, so he devised a contingency plan. When he was assigned to oversee the daily operations of the concentration camps, he made it his personal mission to find a male prisoner who was a similar age, height, and build to his own. Eventually, he found one – Benjamin Goldman, who, in many ways, looked like Hanns's doppelganger.

Hanns took Benjamin under his wing, treating him well and ensuring the guards did the same. He made him his personal office clerk, assigning him various admin tasks and duties. This kept Benjamin away from the hard labour and spared him from the gas chambers.

Over time, Hanns and Benjamin developed mutual feelings for each other, and would often steal glances at one another when they thought no one was looking. Of course, for obvious reasons, nothing ever came of their connection.

Hanns didn't actually agree with Hitler's views on the Jewish people, nor did he fully embrace the Nazi Party's beliefs. Like most Germans at the time, he went along with the regime largely out of fear. In a dictatorship, any hint of nonconformity could result in being labelled an enemy of the state, which would lead to either execution or being sent to a camp. So, like a dutiful SS officer, he did what he was told and followed his orders without question.

Towards the end of the war, Hanns forged identification papers for himself under the name of Benjamin Goldman. He kept these papers on him at all times, and even gave himself a fake prisoner identification number tattoo on his right wrist, which he concealed under his wristwatch.

When Nazi Germany fell, Hanns received orders to exterminate as many prisoners as possible and then flee. He placed the forged identification papers at the back of the prisoner archive folder in his office and set off to find Benjamin. He told Benjamin he was taking him somewhere safe, and he gave the order for his men to exterminate the remaining prisoners before leaving the camp in an SS car, along with his driver.

They headed west towards the advancing Allies and, after a few miles, they found a secluded spot at the edge of a vast field, where the treeline of the forest met the open ground.

Hanns got out of the car and began removing his uniform, instructing his driver to stay alert and keep watch for the Allies. He then ordered Benjamin to strip off his prisoner uniform and go to the trunk of the car, where Hanns had stashed civilian clothes for them both.

Benjamin did as he was told and went to the trunk of the car. However, when he opened the boot, he was stunned to find it empty. Before he could react, Hanns pulled out his Luger and shot Benjamin in the side of the head. The young driver, who'd been standing guard, was startled by the gunshot and turned around to see what had happened. Without hesitation, Hanns aimed the Luger at the driver and shot him as well.

Once the men were dead, Hanns quickly went to work. He removed Benjamin's filthy, smelly, striped prisoner uniform and dressed Benjamin's corpse in his own smart SS uniform. He then removed his wristwatch and fastened it to Benjamin's right wrist.

His plan was now complete – he had assumed the identity of Benjamin Goldman. He would now be seen as a 'Jewish survivor' of the terrible atrocities of the war, a person who had lived through the horrors of the concentration camps – rather than being in charge of them.

Hanns scooped up a handful of mud and smeared it across his face, neck, and arms to give the appearance of someone who hadn't washed for some time. With his skinny, athletic build, he already looked like he could be undernourished.

Next, he placed the Luger in Benjamin's right hand, hoping to make the scene look like a murder-suicide.

Once he was finished, he stood over Benjamin's body for a few moments, staring at the lifeless corpse. A tear formed and rolled down his cheek, but he quickly wiped it away. The blood from Benjamin's wound pooled on the dark, wet mud beneath him.

With one last glance at the body, Hanns set off on foot, walking across the fields for hours.

Eventually, he saw the advancing Allies, and in an act of surrender, Hanns fell to his knees in front of an American Sherman tank, raising his arms and wailing in desperation.

An American GI climbed down from the tank and

wrapped a blanket around him. Hanns then told the soldiers his 'extraordinary story' of escape from the camp.

The Allies turned Hanns over to the Red Cross, and he applied for political asylum in the UK.

With the chaos of post-war Europe – including 65 million displaced people – Hanns managed to slip under the radar. After all, who would have the spine to challenge a 'concentration camp survivor'? Who would ask them to relive the trauma of the past six years of living hell by detailing their experiences?

Hanns took full advantage of this, speaking only when spoken to and never deviating from his cover story.

Later, when Benjamin's body was discovered by the Allies, an investigation was launched. They wondered how a high-ranking SS officer came to have a prisoner identification number tattooed on his right wrist.

However, this investigation was never pursued further, and the corpse was looted of anything of value or significance before being buried in an unmarked grave. The strange tale quickly faded into history, becoming little more than rumour and hearsay.

By this time, Hanns was safely out of Europe and therefore less inclined to look over his shoulder. He made sure his tracks were well covered and he settled into his new life fairly quickly. Apart from the local newspaper running an article on his 'extraordinary survival story,' he kept a low profile. He took a job as an auctioneer and mostly kept to himself, rarely interacting with anyone – aside from exchanging pleasantries with his neighbours.

But behind closed doors, his obsession with the supernatural and witchcraft intensified, especially as he grew older. One day, while at work, he came across an old antique witchcraft book – the *Grimoire*. The very same book he'd been searching for decades earlier.

As he thumbed through its pages, he came across a spell designed to open a demonic portal. His mind raced, his neurons ablaze with all the things he could do with the spellbook. He had to have it. So, ensuring no one was around, he slipped the book into his briefcase and went home for the night.

Once home, he devoured the book, studying every word, diagram, and page from front to back. The book detailed the requirements for performing these devilish witchcraft spells, with a certain mood and atmosphere needing to be set. The room had to be completely dark, and a pictogram – the symbol of the Devil and black magic – had to be drawn in chalk on the floor and wall. Candles had to be strategically placed in specific locations around the room.

Hanns quickly decided on the perfect place to perform the ritual: the attic.

So, with everything in hand, he marched upstairs, prepared to perform the ritual. He lit the candles, positioning them just right, and then drew the pictogram on the exposed bare brick with chalk and bare floorboards.

Once everything was in place, he recited the incantation and successfully summoned a demon through the portal. When the demon appeared before him, Hanns – with unshakable determination – told it that he wished to join it, feeding on souls and living for eternity, switching between the mortal and immortal realms.

Ordinarily, when a demon is summoned by a

mortal, it would simply possess and devour that individual's soul. But Hanns Dietrich Fritz was no ordinary individual, and his evil, sadistic nature was clear for the demon to see.

Impressed by his darkness, the demon agreed to grant his wish – but only on the condition that Hanns make a sacrifice of his own. Hanns was told that in order to seal the pact, he would need to cut off his left index finger while reciting the words of the spell.

The demon produced a sharp, serrated, jagged dagger, about seven inches long, and handed it to Hanns.

Hanns did exactly as instructed, taking the knife and cutting off his finger. He howled in pain as his blood stained the spellbook, then he quickly reached into his pocket and retrieved a handkerchief, wrapping it tightly around his knuckle stump.

The demon, satisfied with Hanns's sacrifice, saw that he was eager for the demonic transformation. So, the demon cast the spell, transporting him to the other immortal realm, where Hanns became an incubus – a hybrid, with all the supernatural abilities that demons possessed.

In an instant, Hanns's appearance completely transformed. He was no longer a flabby 60-year-old man; his body was now lean and toned. His ears had become pointed, his nostrils flared, and his nose flatter. His skin looked as if it had been dyed charcoal – a grim, dirty tone. His teeth had become pointed, though rotten. But most terrifying of all were his eyes: the whites had turned yellow, his pupils became vertical, and his irises were blood red. He was truly a grotesque sight to behold.

As Hanns stepped through the portal, the entire

house shook. A gust of wind rushed through the house, extinguishing the candles. Plasterboard fell from the attic ceiling, covering the chalk pictograms, which would remain hidden for many decades to come.

To the outside world, Hanns – or Benjamin – simply disappeared without a trace. His house and all of his possessions were auctioned off, and a new family moved in.

But David and Jenn knew none of this… yet.

***

David was still shaken by what he'd discovered, the same questions swirling around in his head.

Were these two missing individuals truly supernatural entities haunting his house? If so, why? And, more importantly, how could he rid himself – and his family – of them?

Deep down, David knew he had to tell Jenn everything he'd discovered. But part of him hesitated. She already had enough on her plate, worrying about the results she was waiting to get from the doctor. Or perhaps it was his pride, his silly ego preventing him from admitting he was wrong.

David was between patient visits, and he had about an hour and a half to kill. Usually, he would go back to the office, eat his lunch, and type up his notes, or park up somewhere and do the same in the car. But today was different. With everything going on at home, he felt a burning desire to find some holy water. He didn't feel safe without it.

Fortunately, there was a church just around the corner from one of his patients' houses. So, David got out of his car, walked up to the church, and then took a moment to admire the grand old building. He'd never noticed how beautiful churches really were. The stonework, the weathered stone gargoyles guarding the church from above, the ornate stained-glass windows… everything about it was absolutely stunning.

Maybe it was because he hadn't spent much time around churches. Funerals, weddings, and christenings, sure, but apart from that, he didn't take much notice of them. It was as if he was really seeing them – and understanding them – for the first time.

Shaking himself back to reality, David stepped up to the huge, heavy wooden door and pushed it open.

He walked slowly over the threshold, closing the door quietly behind him. The smell of stale incense hung in the air, mixed with the faint scent of burning candles.

It sounded like a choir was gently singing some kind of Latin hymn, but when David glanced towards the altar, it was empty. Looking up at the grand stone pillars holding up the huge wooden rafters, he noticed several speakers mounted on them. It must be a CD playing through them, he thought.

There were about half a dozen people scattered all around the church. David slowly walked down the aisle, found an empty bench, and quietly sat down. He felt strangely relaxed, and warm – though he wasn't sure why.

His attention was soon drawn to the rows of burning candles in the corner by the confessional box; David knew that people often lit candles for their loved ones who had passed away. *So that's why it's so warm in here*, he thought.

After a while, the other people began to leave, and a priest emerged from his confessional box, looking around. He was an older, heavyset gentleman with greyish-red hair and an equally grey-reddish beard. He appeared to be in his mid-to-late 60s, dressed in the usual holy attire.

He spotted David and smiled, making his way over. Then, sitting down in front of him, the priest said, "Hello, my son, are you here for confession?" He spoke softly, and with a thick Irish accent.

David smiled too. "Not exactly, Father... I was actually looking for some holy water," he said quietly.

"Ah, well, we have plenty of that here," the priest replied. "Is it for a sore throat?"

David's face dropped, a dazed and confused look spreading across his features. "Er... no... it's..."

The priest chuckled to himself. "I'm only joking with you, son. I say that to all the blue-rinse old dears in here. It gives them a laugh – and I love a good laugh," he added with a twinkle in his eye.

David laughed nervously.

"Come with me," the priest said, standing up. "I'll see if I can find you some."

David stood up and followed the priest down the aisle, past the altar, and towards a cupboard in the corner of the church. The priest opened the door and began rummaging through its contents.

"Your church is absolutely stunning, Father," David remarked. "I've never noticed how beautiful these old buildings really are."

"Oh, it's not my church, son. It's God's house. He's

out at the moment – I'm just house-sitting," the priest replied with a chuckle.

David smiled. He liked this old, eccentric gentleman. He made him feel at ease.

After a few more moments of searching, the priest found what he was looking for. He pulled out a small plastic bottle with a blue top and a picture of the Virgin Mary on the front. "Ah, here's some," he said, holding it up. "Just don't get it mixed up with your aftershave… you'll have a coven of nuns chasing after you! That happened to me at Lourdes back in 1983; the sisters go mad for the stuff!" With that, the priest cackled so much that he had to wipe a tear from his eye.

David couldn't help but laugh too. "I'll keep that in mind, Father," he said with a grin, pausing for a moment before explaining, "A friend of mine told me holy water helps ward off evil spirits, so I thought I'd give it a try." He shrugged. "I mean, I've got nothing to lose."

The priest scratched his short beard thoughtfully. "Hmm… are you being visited by spirits, my son?"

David sighed. "Something like that, Father. My family and I have experienced a lot of strange goings-on at home recently. We're not the religious type, I'm afraid, but I thought there's no harm in trying…"

"I see," the priest said, his expression growing more serious. "Well, in that case…" He stepped in front of David, made the sign of the cross, placed his hand on David's shoulder, and closed his eyes. "Dear Heavenly Father," he began, "bless this man and his family. Although they are not part of Your flock, they are in great need of Your guidance. Protect them from all the evil spirits that have come to torment them. Shield them with Your light and guide them through the darkness. May they find peace. In the name of the Heavenly Father, the Son, and the Holy Ghost. Amen."

David looked up, feeling awkward. "Erm... amen... thank you, Father. How much do I owe you?"

The priest held his hand up and smiled. "Nothing at all, my son. Go in peace, and may the holy water bring you and your family everlasting peace and happiness. Come on, I'll walk you out."

David smiled and nodded. "Thank you, Father. That's very kind of you."

They reached the door, and David noticed a table off to the right-hand side. It was a charity donation table for Oxfam, with a collection tin in the centre. He stopped, smiled, and turned back to the priest. Reaching into his pocket, he dug out a five-pound note, held it up to the priest, then folded it neatly and slipped it into the collection box.

The priest smiled and bowed his head in thanks.

"What you give out, you get back, Father," David told him. "Thank you again."

"I couldn't have put it better myself, my son. God bless you. And if you ever need anything else... incense, perhaps, or even just to talk... you know where I am."

They shook hands as David stepped outside, feeling safe – and ready.

As the priest stood at the door, watching David walk to his car, he suddenly spotted something sitting in the back seat that he couldn't quite make out. Then he realised what it was.

"Holy Mary, Mother of God!" he muttered, startled, crossing himself. Then, he grabbed his crucifix hanging around his neck and kissed it. "God help that poor family! Hail Mary, full of grace…" He began to pray, quickly shutting and bolting the heavy wooden door of the church as David drove away.

From then on, David started carrying the holy water and iron shavings with him at all times. As much as part of him tried to deny that spirits and ghosts existed, and even though he was a man of reason, he was starting to see that the evidence spoke for itself. He couldn't explain how or why these things were happening in the house, but he had a feeling that things were going to get a whole lot worse.

So, the holy water and iron shavings couldn't hurt – if anything, it made him feel slightly safer. And he would take as much safety as he could right now.

CHAPTER 13

It was Friday afternoon, and David had just finished with the last of his patients. However, he still had his notes to type up and other various admin tasks to complete.

Matt was sitting at his desk, typing up his own patient notes. He looked up and smiled as David walked in. "Hi, David!" he greeted cheerily. "How are you?"

David smiled back. "Hi, Matt. I'm fine, how are you?"

As David made his way to his desk, Matt replied, "I'm very well, thanks, mate. Just finishing up the last of these notes, then I'll be heading home."

David pulled his chair out from under the desk and collapsed into it. "That's good. I'm going to make a coffee in a minute. Do you want me to make you a cup?"

"No, thanks. I'll be leaving in about five minutes, but thanks anyway."

"No problem," David replied, unzipping his laptop backpack and retrieving the laptop from its cushioned pouch. Opening it up, he sat it in the docking station on his desk and then typed in his username and password to log into the system.

Matt suddenly looked up from his computer. "Oh, I've been meaning to ask, David – how are you getting on at home with your paranormal visitor?"

David looked up, his face dropping.

"That bad, is it?" Matt asked.

"Well," David said, sighing, "since we last spoke, there have been way more strange things happening. I've been having these weird nightmares where I can't move, I've been hearing voices in the house when it's just me, and the kids found a finger in the attic…"

Matt's eyes widened. "A finger?" he asked, incredulous.

"Yeah," David replied, nodding. "A long, black, mummified finger. It looked like it had been there for decades. Probably a work accident or something…"

Matt nodded slowly as David continued.

"And the nightmares I've been having are actually sleep paralysis – I looked it up. It's common if you don't get enough sleep or have a disrupted sleep pattern…"

Matt interrupted him. "And with the voices, is it a voice you've never heard before, or is it a voice you recognise?"

"It was Jenn's voice," David replied. "It was the same day I explained everything to you about what was going on in the house. You know, a few weeks ago."

Matt nodded.

"Well," David continued, "that evening, my mum had the kids for the night, and Jenn had gone to bingo with her mum, so I was alone in the house. I'd just run a bath and got into it, then I heard Jenn calling me. So, I got out of the bath, but there was no one there. I called Jenn on the phone, and she told me she was just about to start her bingo game… She hadn't been in the house at all."

Matt cleared his throat. "So, by the sounds of it, the mimicking had started already… Tell me what happened in your nightmare, David."

It was David's turn to clear his throat. "Well… I was asleep, lying on my back, when I suddenly opened my eyes to see this creepy shadow figure lurking in the bedroom doorway. I could hear the kids playing downstairs but I couldn't move. Next, I began to levitate; I floated across the room to the doorway, where I landed in a heap. Then, this thing came closer to my face…"

"Did this thing speak?" Matt interrupted.

"Yes," David replied. "It said it would…" He paused, shaking his head. "It would take our souls…"

Matt's face dropped, and David could see the concern in his eyes.

David smiled. "But it's just a nightmare, right? I mean, I googled it the next morning, and it said it was just sleep paralysis…"

Matt's tone grew more serious. "It might be, but then again, it might not be. From what you've just told me, David – that you had a nightmare about a creepy shadow figure who threatened to take your souls – I doubt a sceptic would have such a dream, or nightmare. To me, I'd take that as something sinister that's attached itself to you and is clearly letting itself be known…"

David's mouth suddenly went dry. He had just

remembered something. "There's something else…" he said.

Matt nodded at him to continue.

"A few weeks ago, I visited one of my patients. His wife let me in and told me she'd been up all night with him, with a suspected UTI…"

Matt leaned in, listening intently as David continued.

"Long story short, he did have a UTI, and he was hallucinating and very distressed. Anyway, I gave him my phone to show him pictures of my kids, trying to calm him down a bit. I'd just finished taking his obs when he started hallucinating again." He paused for a moment. "Unbeknownst to me at the time, the patient activated the recorder app, and the phone recorded everything. When I got back to the car, I listened to it… and, well…"

Matt frowned. "Well, what, David?"

David sighed, pulling out his phone and walking over to Matt's desk. "Well, it was a bit weird, and I didn't know what to make of it…" He opened the recorder app, found the recording, turned the volume up on the side of his phone, and placed it on Matt's desk.

"Gus, you have an infection at the moment, and your temperature is really high. So, I'm going to call the doctor and see if we can get you admitted to hospital – you'll need some intravenous fluids and antibiotics. OK?"

Matt leaned closer to the phone just as Gus started screaming hysterically.

"Juden… juden… I will take your soul, juden… Golem! Golem! Yes, juden, I am…"

David stopped the recording and slipped his phone back into his pocket.

The colour had drained from Matt's face, leaving him chalk white. Slowly, he sat back in his chair, staring at David in disbelief.

After several moments, Matt cleared his throat. "David… is that the same voice from your dreams?"

David looked down at his feet and nodded.

Matt brought his hands up to his mouth. "Oh my God, David… this shit is the real deal! This isn't just some spirit trying to disrupt your home life…a full-blown demonic entity has attached itself to you!"

By now, David was starting to feel physically sick. "What can I do to get rid of it?" he asked.

Matt thought for a moment. "Well, the first thing you need to do is accept that this is actually happening. I know you're not a believer, David, but this is real. And whatever this thing is, it's not going to stop until it gets what it wants." He sighed loudly. "OK, the next thing you need to do is contact a reputable psychic or medium. They'll be able to help you. For now, go home and sage every single part of your house. Hopefully, that will keep it at bay for the time being – until the psychic or medium can do their thing."

David nodded slowly. "Anything else I can do to try and get rid of this thing?" he asked.

Matt nodded. "Yeah, try and find out everything you can about demonology. You know what they say: Knowledge is power, and know thy enemy and all that. Oh, and if I were you, I'd explain to Jenn what's going on and maybe get them away from the house for a few days."

David smiled. "I will… thanks, Matt," he said as he went back to his desk.

Matt nodded. "Good luck, man. I've got to go now, but keep me posted, yeah?"

"Sure," David said, sitting down and heading straight to Google. "I'll see you soon."

Once Matt had gone, David began googling everything he could about demonology. He also searched for reputable psychics and mediums in the area. David had always been sceptical about these people, feeling they exploited others' grief for their own financial and personal gain… but at this point, he could use all the help he could get.

After a while, he found a woman who lived locally, called her, and explained what was happening. She agreed to stop by the house on Saturday afternoon – the next day – at around 4 pm.

David spent the next hour reading up on demonology, his mind boggling – he couldn't believe what he was learning. He read about everything from religious cults to witchcraft in medieval times. He discovered that demons could live up to 5,000 years and that they imprison and feed on souls through fear. He also learnt about different forms of demons, like the incubus – half human, half demon. There were myths about witches breeding with demons to produce incubus offspring, spreading evil and terror.

However, the most concerning thing David read was that it was nearly impossible to get rid of or defeat a demon.

Then, he came across a link to a famous demonic book called the *Grimoire*, created by Devil-worshipping witches to summon demonic spirits. It was full of spells, curses, and sacrificial rituals.

Intrigued, David copied and pasted the word 'Grimoire' into Google and hit search, frowning when he saw the results. One of the links led to an old newspaper article from 1970. It mentioned that a local auction house, Thompson and Sons, had temporarily been in possession of this particular book. However, it was allegedly stolen by an auction house employee who subsequently went missing. The employee's name was Benjamin Goldman.

David's heart skipped a beat. He remembered that name from the census reports he'd found online. He also recalled the Thompson and Sons receipt book he'd found while ripping out the old kitchen.

He couldn't believe what he was reading. *That's the connection*, he thought. Benjamin Goldman had lived in David's house and worked at the auction house all those years ago.

In that moment, David decided that when he went home that night, he would sit Jenn down and explain everything he'd been experiencing recently. He would also finally admit that she'd been right all along – there was definitely something supernatural going on in the house.

As the afternoon wore on, David finished his work for the day, picked up the kids, and went home to make dinner.

Meanwhile, Jenn was still at work. She was sitting at her desk, scrolling through the pictures on her phone.

Soon, she came across a photo of the four of them on the beach, which made her smile. However, the smile soon faded as something caught her eye – something she hadn't noticed before.

Jenn zoomed in on the picture and studied it for a moment, frowning. There appeared to be some kind of white mist standing just behind David. She swiped through the next few photos, taken by the same woman of the old couple, and examined them closely. They were all exactly the same. The mist didn't shift in any of the frames.

For a moment, Jenn thought it must be the reflection of the sun on the sea or something similar, but she quickly dismissed this explanation. After all, that's the kind of thing David would say.

She pressed and held one of the pictures until it was highlighted, then went into her filter settings and switched it to the negative filter.

Jenn gasped, dropping her phone onto the desk.

The negative filter had turned everything black and white. The white mist around David was now black, and it looked like a shadowy outline of a man standing behind him. It had a head and two arms, and it appeared to be holding onto David's shoulders.

Jenn couldn't believe her eyes.

Just then, her phone rang, startling her. It was her doctor, asking her to come in for an appointment to discuss the results of her scan.

Jenn's heart sank. She knew it wasn't good news – if it had been, the doctor would have given her the all-clear over the phone.

Her mind racing, Jenn finished work early and headed straight to the doctor's surgery. Her worst fears were confirmed: the shadow on her lung was indeed cancerous. In that instant, Jenn's whole world seemed to collapse around her.

The doctor explained the procedures and treatments that were available, but Jenn couldn't focus on any of it.

All she could think about was how she would never watch her two beautiful little girls grow up. She wouldn't get to help them through their first heartbreaks, see them walk down the aisle at their weddings, or hold her grandchildren in her arms. She would never fulfil her retirement plans with David, to travel the world and see all the places she'd always dreamed of seeing.

She had no idea how she was going to break this horrible news to David.

Her mind was racing at 100 miles per hour as she walked out of the doctor's surgery, her steps mechanical as she wandered aimlessly, staring into space. On autopilot, she found her way home and put on a brave face for the kids.

They were sitting at the dining table, eating dinner. She walked over to them, giving them each a big hug and a kiss. Tears welled up in her eyes, but she quickly wiped them away. Then, she walked over to David, giving him a tight hug too.

David could sense that something was up with her, but before he could ask what was wrong, she pulled away and went upstairs to change out of her work clothes. Once changed, she just sat on the edge of the bed and sobbed.

By 8:30 pm, David and Jenn had put the kids to bed. It was a Friday night, the night they usually sat downstairs in the front living room and had a few drinks. This was when David planned to finally admit he'd been a fool and tell Jenn everything he'd been experiencing.

David poured Jenn's drink, grabbed a beer from the fridge for himself, and walked through to the front room, sitting down next to his wife on the couch.

"Jenn," he said, "I need to talk to you about something-"

Jenn held up her hand, stopping him. "David, wait... I need to tell you something first..."

David frowned. "OK, go ahead."

Jenn took a long gulp of her drink, followed by a deep breath. "OK... the doctor called me this afternoon and asked me to come in... so I finished early and went to see him..." Her eyes began to well up.

David cleared his throat. "OK... so what did he say?"

Jenn began to sob quietly.

David put his beer down on the side table next to him, then moved closer to Jenn and wrapped his arm around her. "Jenn... what's going on?" he asked gently, the concern evident in his voice.

"David... I... I have lung cancer," she said, breaking down into uncontrollable sobs.

David's face dropped. He was in shock, unable to process what he'd just heard. He pulled her close and wrapped his other arm around her too. His mind raced with questions, so many scenarios flashing through his head, but in that moment, he did the only thing he could – he held her, comforting her as much as possible.

They sat together for hours, long into the night,

talking and drinking – and crying. Time seemed to slip away. David tried to reassure Jenn that everything would be OK and they would get through it. Jenn wasn't so sure.

Then, after a brief, comfortable silence, Jenn suddenly remembered that David had something to tell her.

She turned to him. "What was it you wanted to tell me earlier, David?"

David smiled, shaking his head slightly. "I… I was… it's nothing important, sweetheart. I can't even remember now…"

He figured she had enough on her plate at the moment; the last thing she needed was to worry about the strange things happening in the house.

***

The next morning – after very little sleep – Jenn decided to take the girls out for a few hours to meet her friend and her two kids for a playdate. She wanted to create as many memories as possible with them, knowing how precious their time together was.

Meanwhile, David had planned to tackle some DIY jobs around the house that he'd been putting off for weeks; he thought it would be the perfect opportunity to take his mind off things – at least until the local psychic woman came around at 4 pm. He just hoped Jenn and the girls would still be out then. His plan for now was to paint the kitchen and dining area white, which he didn't think would take too long – maybe a couple of hours.

However, before he could begin, he needed to patch up a few holes in the walls with some ready-mixed plaster. Then, he'd have to wait for it to dry before giving it a light sanding to smooth away the rough patches, ready to paint.

David went to the garage to gather his tools, rummaging through the drawers where he kept his paintbrushes and other DIY items. He selected a small cutting in brush, a broader brush for the corners, and a roller and tray. He also grabbed dust sheets, the white paint, the tub of patching plaster, and his wallpaper scraper.

Carrying everything back into the house, he set the tin of paint, the roller, and the tray on the table. He moved all the furniture to one side of the room and then covered them with the dust sheets. Next, he opened the tub of plaster and stirred it with his wallpaper scraper until it reached a smooth consistency, before setting about patching up the holes in the wall.

David was so busy concentrating on his task, he didn't notice that Hanns had appeared a couple of feet behind him.

Even when Hanns took a step closer to David, he still didn't realise the figure was there.

With a sinister smile, Hanns took one final step forward, merging with David's body.

David gasped as his whole body went rigid, dropping the wallpaper scraper and tub of plaster. With his arms outstretched and unable to move, his head clicked back until he was staring at the ceiling. He was completely paralysed, just as he'd been in the nightmare a couple of weeks earlier.

He started to hyperventilate. Moments later, David's eyes turned black and he began to levitate. His body twitched uncontrollably, as though he was having a seizure.

Suddenly, David was flooded with visions. He saw everything that Hanns had experienced, everywhere he had been.

He saw himself, unable to move during his nightmare, now through the eyes of Hanns. David watched his own lifeless body levitating in the bedroom on that fateful night. He saw it fall to the ground, landing before the creature's feet.

Another vision flashed before him. This time, he was sitting in the back seat of his car, watching himself drive and stop at some traffic lights. He remembered this moment clearly – this was when he'd seen the entity in the rearview mirror.

Another vision took over. David watched himself getting out of the car, going into the church, and returning some time later. He saw the priest standing outside, crossing himself and hurrying into the church, locking the door behind him.

More images flashed before David's blackened eyes. He saw the girl, Katie, being abducted by Hanns at the mental hospital, followed by the tragic scene of James Maxwell being trapped in the burning house.

David felt sick. He began to vomit, choking on white mucus, still paralysed in his uncontrollable state.

But the visions didn't stop.

David saw the day he visited his patient Gus, when he had an infection and was screaming with fear. The entity was there, standing behind David, taunting him. Then, he saw himself at his occupational health appointment, stuck in the malfunctioning lift that had led him to the basement.

The visions were coming faster now.

He saw the black dog on his driveway, the light switch clicking in the dead of night, the entity creeping into the kids' room while they slept, grabbing at their arms and legs, bruising their soft skin.

The entity had always been with David, watching him, stalking him, and haunting his entire family. Why hadn't he believed Jenn? Why had he dismissed her fears every single time, always turning everything into a joke? Why hadn't he taken her seriously?

Tears welled up in David's eyes and slowly rolled down his cheeks.

Moments later, his body went limp and he passed out, hitting the kitchen floor. He was out cold.

Hanns stepped out of David's body, staring down at him with a sinister smile before vanishing into thin air.

Deliverance.

When David regained consciousness, he found himself lying face down on the kitchen floor. He must have blacked out, he thought, but for how long he didn't know. What he'd seen in those visions had shaken him to his core.

One thing was clear – he had to get his family away from the house, whether or not the psychic managed to do anything. He simply had to get them to safety.

At around 3:45 pm, Jenn and the kids came home, and the girls ran straight upstairs.

"Remember to tidy your room, girls!" Jenn called

after them. "I'll be up in a minute to check if you've done it properly!"

"OK, Mummy!" both girls replied.

Jenn walked into the kitchen and saw David standing in the dining area. "Hey, honey, how are-"

He turned around to face her.

Jenn took one look at him and immediately knew something was wrong. He seemed distressed, dishevelled, and utterly bewildered.

"David, what's wrong?" she asked, her voice breaking. "What's happened?"

He stepped towards Jenn and hugged her tightly.

"David! Seriously... tell me what's going on! What happened?"

David placed his hands on Jenn's shoulders, looked into her eyes, and took a deep breath. "You were right, Jenn... you were always right... and I'm so sorry I brushed you off," he said quietly, not sounding like himself at all.

Jenn frowned. "What are you talking about? You're really scaring me now. Tell me – what the hell is going on?"

"This house, Jenn!" David replied, his voice trembling. "This house and all the creepy stuff that's been happening – the loud bangs in the middle of the night, the things the kids have been seeing, the big black dog, the nightmares I've been having – it's all been him!"

Jenn frowned again. "Who?" she asked, confused.

"The Black Finger Man... the entity... he's been haunting us since we moved in," David told her. "He's attached himself to me, and he wants to take us." He turned away from Jenn and headed for the kitchen cupboard, retrieving his work bag and bringing it back to the dining room table. Opening it, he pulled out a folder containing all the information he'd printed in his office. "A couple of weeks ago, I started looking into the history of this house," he explained. "At first, I was just looking for land registry and census documents, but then I stumbled across these old newspaper articles."

David opened the folder, placing each article down on the table for Jenn to see. "Look, Katie McKinnon. She was 18 when she escaped from a mental hospital – in 1971. She was never seen again. Jenn, this is the girl I've seen on our CCTV."

He pointed to the next page. "James Maxwell. He was a night watchman for a bus depot, and a chain smoker. It's alleged that he died in a fire in 1983, but his body was never found. He's the smoking man, dressed in black, who the girls saw in the garden."

Jenn's hand went to her mouth as she listened, horrified.

David continued, his voice quieter now. "And finally… Andrew Thomas, aged six, went missing from his garden in 1995. Look at the picture, Jenn… do you recognise him?"

Slowly, Jenn picked up the piece of paper and took a closer look. "Oh my God!" she gasped. "That's Andy!"

"That's right," David replied. "Andy is the little boy the girls have been playing with in the garden ever since we moved in! Between the four of us, we've all been seeing and interacting with these spirits."

Jenn's face went pale, her mind racing as she

processed this revelation. After a moment, she frowned and cleared her throat. "But how is this all connected, David? I don't understand."

"Because they all lived in this house."

The hairs on the back of Jenn's neck stood on end as she stared at David, wide-eyed. "I... I have something to show you too," she said, her voice shaky as she went to the kitchen cupboard above the kettle, retrieved the kids' drawings, and handed them to David.

"What are these?" David asked, looking at the pictures.

Jenn sighed. "The kids drew these a couple of weeks ago, remember? Well, this one is new..." She showed him the most recent drawing Bella had made, featuring Andy and the girl she now knew to be Katie.

David studied the drawing, his eyes widening in shock. "Oh my God... why didn't you tell me?" he exclaimed, his voice filled with disbelief.

Jenn scoffed. "What, and have you dismiss me and turn it around, saying I'm overreacting?"

David's eyes were now full of tears; they rolled down his cheeks as he slowly closed his eyes and nodded. "I'm sorry, Jenn... I'm so sorry... I should have listened to you," he whispered, rubbing the tears away with his hands and trying to keep his composure. "Listen... this house is cursed by some demonic entity, and it wants our souls. But I'm not going to let that happen, Jenn... That's why I need you to take the kids and go..."

Jenn's face fell. "Go where? We're not leaving without you, David."

"You have to, Jenn," he pleaded. "This thing is stuck

to me like glue – wherever I go, it comes with me. So, you need to take the kids as far away from me as possible."

Jenn began to cry. "I… I don't want to leave you… I don't want you to face this thing on your own!"

David smiled, gently cupping Jenn's face. "You'll always be with me… My main concern is getting you and the kids away from this place, as soon as possible. I'm so sorry. I shouldn't have dismissed your concerns about this house; I should have listened to you. You have no idea how much I love you, Jenn. You and the kids are my whole world."

The kids came running into the kitchen, excited to see David.

"Daddy!" they cried in unison.

David looked at them both, dropping to his knees and hugging them tightly. His eyes were welling with tears again. "My beautiful girls," he whispered, before pulling away and holding their gaze. "Listen to me, girls. You're both going on a little trip with Mummy, OK? I want you to do everything Mummy tells you to do and help her whenever you can. Can you do that?"

The girls both nodded as the tears rolled down David's cheek.

"Why are you crying, Daddy?" Bella asked.

David quickly wiped the tears away and smiled at them both. "Daddy is crying happy tears because he loves you both so much, and he is so proud of you."

The girls smiled back and hugged him tightly.

David embraced his children, closing his eyes as yet more tears flowed down his face. "Now, listen to me, girls. Don't ever forget how much Daddy loves you, OK? Please don't ever forget. I'll always be with you, forever in your hearts."

"Are you not coming with us, Daddy?" Olivia asked quietly.

David smiled. "Not this time, darling – it's just you, your big sister, and Mummy."

Olivia frowned. "But why? I want you to come."

"I know, darling… I want to come too… but maybe next time."

Tears streamed down Jenn's face as she stood watching David with the girls.

David hugged and kissed them one last time before standing up. "Come on, Jenn, let's get you all out of here…" He picked up Olivia and held her tight, while also taking Bella's hand.

Jenn followed closely behind as they headed for the kitchen door.

Suddenly, the door slammed shut on its own, as though a powerful draught had just swept through the kitchen.

Jenn and the kids gasped in shock. They stood still, frozen for a moment, in utter disbelief.

Slowly, David put Olivia down and reached out for the kitchen door handle while Jenn pulled the kids close to her. Her heart was pounding and sweat was forming on her brow.

David grasped the door handle and tried to pull, but it wouldn't budge. It felt as though an invisible force was holding it shut.

Before he could try again, the kitchen cupboard

doors suddenly flew open, the contents flying out and crashing onto the floor. The girls screamed as pots, pans, dishes, and cutlery scattered across the room. Then, the house began to shake violently.

David stood in front of his family, trying to shield them from the carnage, and turned to Jenn. "Back door!" he shouted. "Go, now!"

Jenn nodded and rushed towards the back door, with the girls close behind.

The house continued to tremble, shaking so intensely that picture frames, mirrors, and even the TV came flying off the wall. The kids were still screaming, absolutely terrified by the nightmare unfolding all around them.

Jenn managed to reach the back door and was just about to grab the door handle when it lifted up of its own accord, engaging the deadbolt with a mechanical *clunk*. She pulled desperately, but the door was locked. Panic gripped her, and she began to cry.

David's heart sank. He knew what he had to do.

With the house still shaking and the kids sobbing in fear, David turned and shouted above the noise of crashing kitchen items and furniture. "Oi! Listen to me!"

The house suddenly stopped shaking, and everything that had been flying around the room dropped to the floor. The girls whimpered as Jenn held them close.

Slowly, David walked into the centre of the room. "It's me you want," he said, his voice steady but strained. "Let my family go, and you can have me… all to yourself…"

For a moment, there was complete silence

throughout the house, a pause in the chaos. Then, an aggressive *thud... thud... thud* banged on the kitchen wall.

David stood tall, resolute. "OK... I'll do you one better," he said. "I formally invite you to take me... just let my family go!"

At that moment, the kitchen door flew wide open, and the front door unlocked with a loud *click*, swinging open by itself.

David turned to Jenn, urgency in his voice. "Go! Now!"

Jenn, sobbing as she held the kids, slowly shook her head. She didn't want to leave David, but she knew she had to keep the girls safe.

"Jenn! Go now!" David shouted desperately.

Reluctantly, Jenn guided the kids out of the kitchen and towards the front door. David stood in the kitchen, watching as his beloved family escaped to safety.

Standing on the doorstep, Jenn paused for a moment and turned back, her gaze meeting David's. Their eyes locked, and he gave her a weak smile before the front door slammed shut and locked itself behind them.

David closed his eyes and let out a heavy sigh. "OK then," he muttered, "let's get this over with... Where do you want me?"

Thud... thud... thud...

The knocks were coming from the hallway, at the bottom of the stairs.

"You want me to follow the knocks?" he asked aloud.

Thud... thud... thud...

David nodded, accepting the inevitable. "Got it," he replied, steeling himself for what was to come.

Chapter 14

David followed the knocking sound all the way up to the attic, stopping in front of the eaves door. He hesitated for just a moment, then pushed it open and crawled in.

His hand scraped along the wall, searching for the light switch in the dark, musty crawl space. Finally, he found it and flicked the switch. The light buzzed to life, dim and flickering, casting shadows across the room. The old fluorescent strip lights sputtered every few seconds, adding an unsettling hum to the air. Despite his fear, David knew exactly what he had to do.

On all fours, he crawled over the decades of forgotten family possessions that were scattered throughout the old attic crawl space. When he crawled past an open box, something caught his eye – an old photograph, a picture of a young girl. Maybe 17 or 18 years old, with long dark hair, she was smiling at the camera, standing in their back garden.

"Oh my God," David muttered under his breath, picking it up. It was Katie McKinnon, the girl who'd gone missing, the one he'd seen on the CCTV footage months before. His blood ran cold and, for a moment, his heart pounded loudly in his chest.

The lights flickered again, snapping him back to reality.

He carefully placed the photo back in the box and carried on crawling towards an open area that was free of clutter.

At the far end of the eaves, David found a brick wall separating the attic from the neighbouring house. It was darker at this end, and he couldn't make out much, so he pulled out his phone and activated the torch, pointing it at the wall.

David gasped when he saw what was on the floor and the bare brick wall. There, drawn in chalk, was a large pentagram – one of the most well-known symbols of Devil worship. He studied it for a moment, his mind racing, before looking around the area. Then, he found it. Tucked beneath one of the old wooden boards, half-hidden in the loft insulation, was the *Grimoire* demon spellbook. Staring at it, his heart skipped a beat.

Crawling closer, he placed his phone on the ground, its torchlight illuminating the space around him. Now on his knees, he hesitated before reaching for the book, his hands trembling.

Slowly, he picked up the dusty book, blowing off the grime that had accumulated on its cover. It had a damp, musty smell to it. Then, slower still, he opened the book, letting his thumb glide over the brittle pages. When he reached the centre of the book, he noticed something that made his stomach lurch: the pages were stained with what looked like dried blood.

At the bottom of one of the pages, some terrifying words were scrawled in dark ink:

'Make a sacrifice while reciting the sacred words…'

"What the fuck?" David whispered, his mind reeling. "What kind of sacrifice?"

The lights at the end of the eaves flickered, then abruptly went out. A soft, shuffling sound echoed behind him, and he froze, his heart hammering in his chest. A second later, the lights flickered back on, casting long shadows across the attic.

Suddenly, something rolled by David's right knee, his eyes slowly moving to see what it was. He gasped.

It was a finger. A long, black, mummified finger. The very same finger the kids had found – the one David had thrown in the bin outside.

"Remember this?" a voice with a thick German accent asked from behind him. "It was my sacrifice."

David's body jolted in shock. He could smell the same putrid stench from his nightmare. His throat tightened, and he closed his eyes, taking a deep, steadying breath. He knew he had no choice but to turn around and face this thing.

So, slowly, David turned, sitting with his back to the wall. He was trapped. There was no way out now, nowhere else to go. Now, he simply had to confront the creepy-looking entity that had been haunting him and his family for months.

There it was, crouched on all fours, the entity staring back at him, their eyes locked.

David tried to clear his throat, the dry, parched

feeling making it difficult to get any words out. "I'm not afraid of you," he said, trying to sound confident.

"Your heart rate and elevated stress levels tell me otherwise," came the calm reply, accompanied by a smile.

David looked the beast up and down. "What the hell are you?" he demanded.

Hanns smiled wider, his lips pursed as he stepped closer. "The Native Americans would call me a Skinwalker," he said. "The ancient Europeans called me a Shifter. The Jews would call me a Golem – a demon – and so on… the list is endless. I, myself, prefer to be called a Shifter."

David narrowed his eyes. "My kids call you the Black Finger Man."

Hanns smiled knowingly. "Just so…"

David's eyes were drawn to Hanns's left hand and his missing index finger. "I assume it was you that killed my cat… in dog form?" he asked, his voice trembling despite his attempts to stay calm.

Hanns held David's gaze and nodded.

"That explains why Jenn couldn't see you on the CCTV," David continued.

Hanns chuckled. "Yes, that is correct."

David's mind was racing. He knew what needed to happen, yet he felt like he should stall this monster in front of him for as long as possible – just in case. "So, what part of Germany did you come from then, Ben? Or do you prefer Benjamin?" he asked, trying to sound confident.

Hanns raised his eyebrows. "Now that's a name I haven't heard in a very long time," he replied with a slow smile. "My real name is Hanns Dietrich Fritz, and I was born in Munich. I was an officer in the German Army during the Second World War. When the war ended and my services were no longer required, I settled here – and the rest, as they say, is history."

"But why would a Nazi officer use a Jewish alias?" David asked, confused. "Who was Benjamin Goldman?"

Hanns cleared his throat, his gaze darkening slightly as memories flashed across his face. "I was not a real Nazi, so to speak," he said, his voice colder now. "I did not believe in the Nazi ideologies. I was never antisemitic. Honestly, I couldn't care less about politics back then. I just did as I was told and followed my orders to the letter."

"And Benjamin Goldman?"

A distant look crossed Hanns's face as he recalled his time in the camp. "Benjamin Goldman was… an… associate of mine. He died towards the end of the war. I merely adopted his identity. When I was found by the Allies, I was turned over to the Red Cross and spent a year or so in a displacement camp. Eventually, I applied for asylum here in the UK."

David scoffed, anger rising within him. "So, you stole a prisoner's identity and then wandered off into the sunset to live happily ever after? Hiding in plain sight?"

Hanns smirked. "You could say that…"

David just stared at him, waiting him out.

"I'm impressed, David," Hanns continued. "You really have done your homework, haven't you? You know, out of all my past subjects, I must say, you're the most inquisitive."

David didn't flinch. "Yes," he replied, his voice steady. "You could say I've been doing my homework on you and your type."

"Is that so?" Hanns asked, grinning.

"Yes. I know that you can live up to 5,000 years. I also know that you survive by imprisoning and feeding on souls – through fear."

Hanns grinned even wider, his lips curling with amusement.

"I also know that you can't be stopped or killed."

"Bravo," Hanns replied, with a mocking clap. "I'm impressed. However," he continued, "you have been incorrectly informed on one or two points. I can live for as long as the gateway to hell is open… So, you could say I can live for eternity, as the gateway will never close. And lastly, I don't devour souls to survive. I feed on souls for power."

David raised his eyebrows, cleared his throat, and took a deep breath, ready to deliver his closing statement. "Well, I know one other thing: holy water and iron shavings can temporarily harm you."

"Is that so?" Hanns asked, his expression unreadable.

David nodded. "And how do I know this? Because I know you're not a real demon."

Hanns's face dropped and, for a moment, David saw a flicker of something unspoken in his eyes.

"You're just an incubus, a half-breed, a hybrid…" David continued.

"But still just as powerful!" Hanns interrupted, stretching out his arm.

In an instant, David felt a strong force tighten

around his neck, like someone was throttling him, yet Hanns was at least five feet away.

Hanns raised his arm higher and David began to rise off the floor, the creature edging ever closer. David reached into his back jeans pocket and grabbed a handful of iron shavings. Hanns was now mere inches from David's face.

David was starting to feel light-headed as his vision blurred, his eyes bulging and bloodshot. After taking a deep breath in an attempt to steady himself, he then reached out and smashed the shavings into Hanns's face.

Hanns let out a terrifying, blood-curdling scream as the iron shavings hissed and melted into his skin.

David fell to the ground, gasping for air as he was released from Hanns's grip. He collapsed on his side and battled to catch his breath while Hanns fell on his back, holding his face. While Hanns was distracted, David reached into his other pocket, pulled out the plastic bottle of holy water, flicked the cap open, and squirted it all over Hanns, who continued to writhe and scream in pain as his skin melted and hissed.

David was just trying to figure out his next step when Hanns burst into flames.

Shocked, David paused for a moment before throwing the last of the iron shavings onto the fireball that had now engulfed Hanns, the shavings hissing and popping as they landed.

While Hanns tried desperately to extinguish the flames by rolling from side to side in such a small space, David saw his chance. He crawled quickly towards the eaves entrance.

As he neared the attic door, however, he felt an invisible force take hold of his body, paralysing him. He collapsed face-first onto the floor, unable to move.

A moment later, he heard movement behind him. Hanns had caught up with him.

The force slowly rolled David onto his back, leaving him completely helpless.

Hanns stood over him, enraged. His face was now severely disfigured, his body smouldering and oozing a thick black substance. David assumed it was demon blood.

The creature then knelt down over David, breathing heavily. "That was a very unwise move," he snarled. "I will enjoy making your final moments on this earth excruciatingly painful."

David cleared his throat. "I don't doubt that," he said softly, "but another thing I know about your kind is that you can't resist a good old-fashioned bargain. A 'deal with the Devil,' so to speak."

A slow smile spread across Hanns's face. "This much is true. Tell me... what is your proposition?"

"Given your powers as an incubus," David told him, "I'm guessing one of the powers you have is to take away and remove illness and disease?"

Hanns frowned, confused. "Of course, though I don't usually do this until after I have imprisoned a soul. You see, illness and disease are like seasoning on a meal to me."

"OK, in that case... I will gladly give you my soul on two conditions," David said, his voice steady. "One, you let my family go, and two, you take my wife's lung cancer away. Completely."

Hanns laughed, confused. "You would willingly give your soul for others?"

David returned the confused look. "Of course I would. I love my family; I would do anything to protect them."

Hanns looked away for a moment, gazing into the corner of the room. "I do not understand this concept. This… is an emotion I have never experienced before."

"You've never been in love before?" David asked quietly.

Hanns hesitated, his thoughts drifting back to the war and his time with Benjamin. He glanced down at his right wrist and saw Benjamin's prisoner tattoo number. He paused before replying, "I… I don't know. I can't recall."

"You mean you've never done something for someone out of compassion or kindness?" David asked. "When you were human?"

Hanns flashed back to the moment he shot Benjamin in the head, feeling a rush of guilt and shame. He closed his eyes, shaking his head to erase the image. He then looked back down at David, who was still lying on the floor, paralysed. "No!" he snapped. "I have never been prone to your mortal emotions, nor did I ever want to be!"

David's voice softened. "Then I genuinely feel sorry for you. I can't even begin to imagine what a dark and lonely existence you've led…"

This enraged Hanns even more. "I don't want your

pity or sorrow!" he shouted. "All I want is what you've proposed. So, do we have an agreement?"

David nodded. "Yes, my soul in exchange for my family's safety, and you take my wife's cancer."

The invisible force lifted, and David regained control of his body. Slowly, he raised his right hand up to Hanns.

Smiling, Hanns reached down to take David's hand in his. "Deal," he growled as he helped David to his feet.

The two of them shook hands, finalising the pact.

Hanns's smile grew wider. "This is a first for me," he said, studying David. "Usually, when I select my subjects, they are terrified for their lives. They scream, they beg. Their fear is intoxicating. But you… I can still smell your fear, but there's also a hint of bravery and a dash of pride. I never thought I would encounter a subject who was actually willing to give me their soul."

David smiled weakly. "Well, there's a first time for everything, I suppose."

Hanns smiled back. "Hmm… indeed. Bear with me, David. I will be back momentarily."

In a reddish-black flash, Hanns disappeared, reappearing behind Jenn, who was standing in her mum's kitchen, staring out of the window towards the back garden. Hanns stepped into her body, temporarily possessing her. Jenn's body jerked, her arms flailing, before going stiff. A moment later, Hanns stepped out of her, vanishing into a dark mist.

Jenn's legs buckled and she fell to her knees, gasping for breath. She felt… strange, almost healthy. The tickly, scratchy sensation at the back of her throat was now gone.

As her breath steadied, she stood up again, wondering what had just happened. *That was weird,* she thought.

Hanns reappeared in the attic as suddenly as he had vanished. "It is done," he said.

David nodded, closing his eyes and inhaling deeply.

While David's eyes were still closed, Hanns clasped a heavy metal collar around his neck, letting the rusty black chain that was attached to it fall to the floor. The weight of it almost caused David to collapse, but he managed to steady himself, standing tall.

"It is time," Hanns declared.

David nodded slowly. "I have one last request."

Hanns turned to face him. "And that is?"

David cleared his throat. "Can I see Jenn one last time?"

Hanns considered the request for a moment, then nodded.

With a flash of bright red light, Hanns and David vanished from the attic.

Just then, outside the house, a woman walked up to the front door and knocked, shivering a little at the dark vibrations she could feel pulsing from the building. She took her sage out of her bag, ready to get to work.

She was running a little late for her 4 pm appointment, but she hoped it wouldn't matter.

Epilogue

Three months had passed, and Jenn had reported David as a missing person. The police, however, weren't particularly interested in investigating his disappearance; they just filed the report and assured Jenn they would notify her if he turned up.

Jenn knew better. She knew the truth. She knew David had sacrificed himself to save her and the kids. Deep down, she knew he was never coming back, though a part of her could still feel his presence lingering around the family.

In those three months, Jenn had put the house up for sale, accepting the first offer that came along. She wasn't interested in getting the best price for the house; she just wanted to get rid of it. What was supposed to be their forever home no longer felt right without David there, and besides, most of the memories she had in that house were filled with pain and fear. She bought a small flat close to her parents, with the proceeds of the the sale of the house

Unsurprisingly, David's disappearance had affected

the girls deeply. They both missed their daddy terribly, and couldn't understand why he wasn't coming home. Staying in the house only made their grief more unbearable. A fresh start was what they needed, Jenn thought.

Angela, too, was devastated by David's disappearance. Jenn had explained everything they'd experienced in the months leading up to David vanishing, and Angela took comfort in the thought that David had given his life to save his family, hoping he was able to find peace in the afterlife with his father. Angela and Jenn continued to support each other through their grief.

Soon after David disappeared, Jenn received the news that she was officially cancer-free, which baffled and astonished the doctors. She was a medical miracle. But, despite her miraculous recovery, she couldn't help feeling that it was all for nothing without David in her life.

She knew, however, that she had to remain strong for her girls.

Jenn went back to work as soon as she could. She couldn't bear the thought of being in the flat alone all day.

Meanwhile, after David went missing, Matt reached out to Jenn. He told her everything David had confided in him regarding the strange occurrences in the house. Jenn, in turn, shared everything she'd experienced, and gave Matt the kids' drawings and the old newspaper articles David had printed out.

Matt was astounded as he sifted through everything, and right then and there, he made a decision: He would pursue a part-time career as a paranormal investigator, or – as David would have called it – a 'Ghostbuster.' Matt smiled to himself as he thought about it, ready to take on the challenge.

A few months later, after completing his investigation in his spare time – and with Jenn's permission – Matt went to the local and national newspapers to share the peculiar tale of David's disappearance, including how the house was connected to various missing persons cases across many time periods. It was met with the usual scepticism, as Matt had predicted.

However, one person who believed the story to be true was the old priest who had gifted David the holy water. He sat in his rectory office, reading the article and staring at David's picture. "That poor family!" he muttered to himself. "May God watch over his wife and children."

The priest then reached for a pair of scissors, cut the article out of the paper, and retrieved a large, old photograph album from his desk drawer. Inside were obituaries of his parishioners who had passed away. He gently lifted the plastic sheet that held the articles in place, placed David's article in the centre of the page, and let the sheet roll back over it.

The priest sighed heavily as he stared at the page for a moment, before putting the album away.

***

Jenn was alone in the office, sitting at her desk and typing up some notes. The office was in a large, old, and very tired council building, and her department consisted of one big room with many desks. Jenn's desk sat next to a window, and on the window ledge sat an old radio that the staff turned on every morning – the music helped with the mundane routine of the office. In the corner of the office, diagonally across from Jenn's desk, was a very old and tired filing cabinet.

Jenn wasn't really paying attention to the radio until she heard what the DJ had just announced: "OK folks, up next, another '80s classic from the legendary band Madness with their cover of 'It Must Be Love.'"

Jenn's ears pricked up, and she stopped what she was doing immediately. As the opening chords began to play, her eyes started welling up. It was her and David's song.

She began to sob quietly as she reached into her bag for a packet of tissues. "It's our song, David!" she whispered as she smiled weakly. "I just wish you were here. I miss you so much."

Just then, one of Jenn's colleagues came into the office, startling her.

"Jenn, I have one of your… Are you OK?" she asked, concerned.

"Hi Denise," Jenn replied. "Yes, I'm fine – just having an emotional moment. Take no notice of me."

Denise gave Jenn a sympathetic look.

"What can I do for you?" Jenn asked as she composed herself and dabbed her tears away with the tissue.

"I have one of your clients downstairs, and they're a bit upset and looking for some advice. Do you want me to tell them you're unavailable?" Denise asked.

Jenn shook her head. "No, not at all. I'll be right down – just give me a minute," she said with a smile.

Denise nodded, smiled back, and walked out of the room, leaving Jenn to get herself together.

Taking a deep breath, Jenn retrieved her compact mirror from her bag and checked her eyes, making sure her makeup was OK. She then screen-locked her computer, stood up, and adjusted her top.

She headed for the door just as the Madness song was finishing on the radio, with the lyrics: *"Nothing more, nothing less... love is the best..."*

Jenn stopped, turned around, and looked at the radio, smiling. "It certainly is," she whispered before walking out of the room.

Time worked differently in the spirit realm. For David and Hanns, they had just left the attic in a flash and arrived in Jenn's office three months later. And, unbeknown to Jenn, David had been standing by the filing cabinet, watching her. His eyes were filled with tears.

"I love you too, sweetheart," he whispered. "I'll always be with you."

Hanns stood next to David. He raised his right arm to David's eyeline, twiddling his long fingers in the air as if he was tuning an invisible radio knob. The radio on the window ledge by Jenn's desk began to crackle and hiss until it stopped on another station.

As the opening chords to 'Sympathy for the Devil' by The Rolling Stones began to play, David closed his eyes, a single tear rolling down his cheek.

"Please allow me to introduce myself, I'm a man of wealth and taste..."

"This is more to my liking," Hanns announced with a smug grin on his face.

David turned to Hanns. "That doesn't surprise me; this song could have been written just for you."

Hanns's grin widened as he nodded. "My thoughts exactly," he said arrogantly.

David turned his back on Hanns to see if he could get a glimpse of Jenn one more time, but Hanns pulled the heavy chain that was connected to David's neck brace, making him wince and stagger under the weight of the brace and chain.

Slowly, David turned back to Hanns. Hanns looked David up and down. David looked Hanns straight in the eye.

"I think I've been more than reasonable, David," Hanns said, pursing his lips. "After all, you got to see her one last time."

David took a deep breath, sighed loudly, and slowly nodded his head. "OK, let's get this over with then."

Hanns smiled, clicked his fingers, and – with a bright red flash of light – they were back in the attic of the house.

David jumped at the sight before him: There were dozens of people sitting on the floor, huddled together, all wearing metal neck braces with thick heavy chains just like David's. As he slowly scanned the room, he spotted Katie McKinnon sitting next to Andy, her arm around him. They were both staring blankly into space, Katie gently stroking his head. David also spotted his old patient Gus, and James Maxwell, the man the kids had seen in the garden. The rest of the people, he didn't recognise.

He looked to his right and saw a pile of chains and neck braces pushed into the far corner of the attic. Hanns had been very busy.

Some of the people were barely visible, as if slowly

vanishing with time, just outlines of their bodies perceptible – like ghosts. Others had missing limbs. By the looks of it, Hanns preferred to devour his captured souls slowly over time.

David turned to Hanns. "Surely, all of these people didn't live here, in this house?" he asked.

Hanns smiled. "Of course not," he replied. "With all of my subjects, I attach myself to them, and they take me with them wherever they go. So, I take their friends, or friends of friends, and so on. That's how I collected your dear patient Gustavo…"

David turned to look at Gus, who was sitting on the floor, also staring into space. His stomach churned when he saw that one of his hands was missing. "So, how do you select your 'subjects,' Hanns? Do you have a special criteria?"

Hanns grinned. "I can see darkness, pain, and sadness in people's souls – these, to me, are the sweetest of delights. For instance, your old friend Gus… his pain was not having any children to call his own." Hanns raised his arm and pointed at Katie. "And young Katie over there, she was in a great deal of pain and sadness due to the sudden death of her mother…"

David interrupted, "And what about Andy over there? What pain and sadness could a child's soul possibly possess?"

Hanns turned to David with an almost troubled look on his face. "Young Andrew was neglected by his parents, emotionally and mentally. His father was a workaholic, and his mother wasn't cut out to be a mum. However, from my experience with young Andrew, I tend not to select children much anymore. They don't have much life experience…"

David looked around at all the sad faces in the attic as Hanns continued.

"And finally, I selected you because you have carried the pain of losing your father from a young age."

"I see," David sighed.

"I like to think of myself as a hunter, a collector of sorts," Hanns said smugly.

"Personally," said David, "I think you're more like a predator, who preys on the weak and the helpless."

Hanns's face dropped; he didn't like that comment. "Well, I guess that would be your prerogative," he sneered.

David turned back to the poor, sorry souls huddled together on the floor. "If we are all your prisoners," he said to Hanns, "why did my family and I see some of these poor souls, like Katie, on the CCTV? And Andy – he used to play with my kids in the garden."

Hanns shrugged. "My subjects are free to roam the house and the grounds as often as they please… they just can't leave the property. Ever. They also can't visit loved ones in the living world, or pass over… not until I'm finished with them, that is…"

An ice-cold shiver slid down David's spine as he turned back to Hanns. "So, in other words, you've created your own purgatory. You have built the worst prison imaginable, where escape is unheard of, and suicide is impossible!"

Hanns smiled widely, smugly. "Just so. Now,

please… make yourself comfortable…" He motioned for David to go and sit down with the others.

David sat down next to Gus, who had only just noticed David was there. He smiled and put his arm around David.

Slowly, Hanns walked to the attic door. Then, with one hand on the handle, he turned around to face his subjects, staring at David and grinning. "Welcome home," he said sinisterly as he slowly closed the door behind him.

Darkness enveloped the poor, enslaved souls imprisoned in the attic, as they agonisingly awaited their fates to be sealed…

Purgatory, it would seem, was as bleak as it sounded.

The End.

Acknowledgements

To Mark and Lorna, thank you for all of your hard work with formatting of the book and cover design. You were both very kind, patient and made me feel at ease. I hope to work with you both again in the future and for many years to come

To Jessica, thank you for editing the book. You did a great job, and helped me give the storyline more depth. I look forward to working with you again in the future.

To Alistair, thank you for all of your advice, tips and guidance, your "nuggets of wisdom" were very much appreciated. Hopefully our paths cross again in the future.

To my beautiful long suffering Wife, thank you for being you! You have always been my spine and my that holds me up, the breath in my lungs, the glue that holds our crazy, mentally deranged family together. More importantly, thank you for giving me OUR beautiful girls. They definitely take after you, and that I would never change.

To my three beautiful, crazy Daughters, you all drive me absolutely mental at times, but I would never change any of you for the world! Thank you for being patient with your daddy while he was unmedicated. Please don't ever forget daddy loves you all, always and forever.

To my Mum, thank you for always believing in me and my passion for writing. And also paying for the editing of this book, I'll bung you a few quid from the royalties…if I ever get any that is!

To my Brother, I know in my younger years, I wasn't the best version of myself and I'm sorry for that but thankfully, I've finally evolved and grown into the best version I can be. You've always been my hero ever since we were young, unfortunately we grew apart. However, I'm glad we're getting there now.

To my Dad, it took me years to realise what it meant to be a man and how to take care of his family. You weren't always there, but you were always there at the right time when I needed you, and they are the times I will always cherish.

I know your memories can be fractured and displaced at times, but I can still remember the happy ones for the both of us.

In our garden of memories, we'll meet again. I'll see you there.

www.ingramcontent.com/pod-product-compliance
Ingram Content Group UK Ltd.
Pitfield, Milton Keynes, MK11 3LW, UK
UKHW010633170625
6432UKWH00029B/87